The

Hangman's

Turn

By A E Johnson

Published by A E Johnson, Little Avalon, Nottingham.
www.authoraejohnson.wordpress.com
contact cammbour@mail.com

Chapter One, Billy

*H*e was hanged by the neck until he was dead. The other flailed like a struggling carp on the end of a line. I had no feelings for these men, what they did took the evillest of courage I had ever seen. The girl they took was left battered; her face was hardly a face after what they had done to her.

I took court the day of their trial, as they stood smug in the dock, waiting for their punishment. Their blackened teeth sunk to a grim realisation that their maker would not welcome them into the kingdom of heaven. The judge that day was kind to fate, their sentence was gratefully carried out by me.

I take no pleasure in death, justice is my pleasure. Seeing the soul drift from their swinging corpses gave me a rare feeling of gladness.

I sit alone in my duty. My family is all I have. Everyone wants to be friends with the hangman, a friendly nod in passing crowds. A pie delivered to the gaol every-so-often, but no one wants to talk to him. I hear no secrets, no lies, the town gossip is left to the wife, Isabelle. A wonderful woman, she puts up with a lot. No wife should have to scrub blood and filth from her husband's clothes, but she does. Without fear or question.

The day I met her, I felt her strength and fell from that moment. My father insisted that love grows, 'tis not something you can expect to see at once. My father, the noble man, and sadly a liar. My love for Isabelle grows each day, from the moment my eyes met hers.

The grim call of the bell at St Peters calls me home each evening. The streets echo with the sounds of those bells, counting our hours, our days, until our final judgement. The cold cobbles beneath the boot gives off the stench of beasts from Market Hill. The town of slaughter sleeps each night upon my return home.

I provide all I can for my family, but debt has hung over us for too long. Our humble home keeps us warm and our bellies full. I regret each day I see the old brown battered door. I could afford more, but in my youth as a worker on the canals, I found a friend in gambling.

Work had days of scarcity, the devil took advantage, but my faith in God is stronger than ever, and now I work to pay my debt and one day see my family in comfort.

The door of the humble home was darker each night I returned. A loud squeal from the hinges alerted Isabelle to my return as she slaved in the kitchen.

'I shan't ask of your day, Love, I know it was a tough one.' Her soft voice sooths me, inviting me into our meagre kitchen.

'Twelve years old.' I heard myself speak, but the strength it had taken was still with me. It was still there, fresh. I could see the boy's face as he turned purple on the end of the rope. His glistening face filled with tears shone in the light of the mid-afternoon sun.

'Father,' called Bethany, my little angel, long flowing hair, just like her mother, the face of an angel, but a dirty angel, she must have been playing in the courtyard with her brother.

'Father,' called Geoffrey. He's a hefty lad, just like his dad, but his mind is tainted by his father's work. 'Did Timothy go quietly?'

A scowl caught my attention. That question pierced me, but I couldn't let him see.

'Now, Geoffrey.' Isabelle scolded him, punishing him for speaking of such things.

'I warned you, when your father returns you speak nothing of it, 'tis not our business, neither is it your father's, so away with you, clean up before dinner.'

The children ran towards the well. I tried to appear joyful, forcing a smile to my face was painful. A sinking pain inside was something she could always see. Wrapping her tiny arms around my waist, she held me tight.

'I know you do all you can for this family.' Her gentle voice and weak frame frightened me. I watched men cry on their final hour, beg me for mercy, and I never broke, but Isabelle, her smile alone shattered me.

I could see a tear struggling to fall from her eye. I rarely show emotion myself. I had become too hardened by my duty.

'I apologise for the poor day you're having. Perhaps the night will see the children to bed early, and we can spend the night by the fire.'

Her growing smile warmed me; her dazzling eyes warmed the cold and desolate world.

'Well, Love, I have an early start on the morrow, I'll see how the evening fairs.' I don't know why I said that; she's offering herself on a plate to me, but all I can see are those struggling eyes.

I don't dream anymore, it's a more swirling nightmare. I don't see the faces of those people on the end of the rope, but I see myself on the end of it; the nightmares never show light, never a day goes when I do not see some iniquitous side of villainous humanity.

I question myself often, I was given this title by God, and that is what I must follow, but when I received this title, it was a tattered old man in a gown who gave it to me, he certainly wasn't God, so how did God give him the right.

When I think of judgement, I wonder who gives a judge the right to bestow punishment on another human soul? How can it be, at just thirty years old, I have already killed over fifty people in our town, and not one person looks to me as a killer. I am a deliverer of justice, but a killer, nonetheless.

The moonlight pouring through the window cast a silver outline down her small figure; she was my queen, and I her king, but in a world so tainted by crime, I needed a new throne, I could no longer bear the thought of my family being judged by Francis Monrow, a man so crooked his own mother would not avoid punishment were a shilling offered.

A cold winter rain covered the streets, hissing from the clunking wheels of the early morning carts as they passed me in the street, sent cold shivers up my spine. Rushing through the streets, the traders ready to start their day tipped hats towards me and others. One foot after another, I can't stop rushing, fearing my body would freeze and take me away from the godforsaken place.

Echoing through the streets, the bells of St Marys gave a single boom, St Peters rang dull that morning, giving a single toll, telling us to hurry to begin our days' graft.

Arriving at the gaol, the moans rang from the cells, covered by the thick wall. Groans and calls from the protests of the Luddites stirred the smoky morning air.

I did my morning rounds, checking that the damned were still there, checking their misery matched mine.

I came unto my duty as an unfeeling, callous man. Isabelle was expecting with Geoffrey. We needed the money. Seeing farming going downhill since the mills moved in, in 1801, I made the hard choice to follow the crowds; we gathered in the towns and cities to find work, the canals did not last long. I found the gaol. It offered me a lifeline while offering so many others' death.

I took the advice of Isabelle's father, Roderick, who suggested we make our mark on the town. I don't think he ever thought his little girl would be living with a killer, and my mark would swell the town with blood.

Population increases saw many come in their droves, and among every one of them, was a criminal waiting to be found.

Walking along the grey stone gaol was a ritual, heading towards the end block where I would collect the day's papers, dress, and ready myself for a day of hanging. 'Twas always a surprise for me to see the names of the condemned.

As soon as I saw it my heart sank, my legs weakened; another child scheduled to die that day, squeezed in at the last minute by the arsehole of a judge, Frank Monrow.

The town changed daily, it grew with industry, but where factories took over, people's homes were destroyed, arguing with wealth saw many to the gaol. The children of the poor often lined doorways in the early morning, before their day of begging began.

I welcomed the children in the gaol. It would mean a warm meal for them, a partial education, something my children were lucky to receive. When the children's wing filled, the normal population would welcome them, where they would not be so lucky. Perhaps death would be a blessing to some. Placed back in the arms of God, would allow a better future.

Now in his sixties, Francis didn't have children. He had never known the love a child could bring. Money was his only thought, his only desire. Rumours spread in the gaol like lice. Francis was often at the forefront of those rumours. He was trusted by men with wealth, others could see the darkness in his dead eyes.

The transportation routes were crowded with Luddites, being sent to a foreign land for standing up for what they believed in. My opinion matters for nothing. I am a gaoler, a hangman, I am nothing.

But here we have the day it changes. I am a man of God, God's children need me. Children, fresh from the dock, thrown to the gallows for the pleasure of sick and twisted men.

The children's hangings were often private, they didn't like a calling crowd. Walking through the cold corridors of the prison, my duties were clear, seeing all those before the gallows, making sure they knew their lines, making sure that their death would be dignified, but it never was.

They all had a distinct look. I knew the fighters, those who would protest their innocence until their dying breath. The fearful, the ones who remained so silent, you doubted they even had a voice at all. Then there were my favourite sort, those of acceptance, the ones who - regardless of their guilt - knew they were about to die, and with that, they would usually place a face upon the situation, making a mockery of everything they could, I knew it was nerves.

I had one man once, he followed everything I said, every instruction he took perfectly, upon talking to a friend of the family when in town, I discovered, it was because he was not like the rest of us, a fall when he was a child would've seen him in an asylum, but his parents kept him free from that, much to the disagreement of the neighbours, they didn't like the look of the boy, he had the mental age of a baby, their hate for the poor boy saw him to my rope, and he did as asked, because his parents told him, 'Be a good boy, and you get a treat later.' He thought they would take him to see the cows on the edge of town. I just hope that little John is in his own field now, filled with all the cows he could ever wish to see.

The children's area of the gaol differed, the stench fills the nose quicker, the poor souls were often left for days, a pen and ink, a sheet of paper, they would write lines constantly, talking of the crime they supposedly committed. One thing about the children's wing was the ever-present feeling of being watched. The ghosts of those babies wandered those halls night and day, waiting for their parents, for someone to collect them, and take them away from the hell of Nottingham town.

The gaol hardened my soul, my own fatherly instincts softened me, I often had to forget I was even a father at all. I wanted to save all of them. Children were naughty, 'twas what God intended, and why we were placed as their parents, to teach them. The sad souls I often found in the gaol had lost their parents long ago. If death hadn't taken them, some other vice had.

Peering through the peephole Billy's cell shattered me. The tiny child was a genetic mess of poor parenting skills. Not a morsel of meat on his living corpse. His smile freed me from my guilt as he looked at the peephole.

I clunked open the heavy wooden door, enough to keep a bull from bolting. This child was smaller than some lice I'd seen crawl from sailors.

Stepping inside my body sank, 'twas a child I was speaking to, I didn't need the authority most adults commanded.

'You, William?' I pointed towards him with my baton.

'Sir.' He nodded his head. He didn't sound like the others in the town. He sounded like he came from good breeding.

'Stand up, boy,' I said to him, as gently as I could. 'Let me see all of you.'

William slowly stood from his chair. His shaking hands were blue from the cold. His innocent eyes looked at me, and then he asked it, the question which changed my life for good.

'Am I to your liking, Sir? I can be a good boy; I swear I won't shout.'

I felt vomit in my mouth. The boy had seen more monsters than I ever would.

'What has you in here, boy?'

'I got caught, Sir.' Straight away I knew something was odd. In my years as a hangman, I was yet to find a guilty man in the gaol.

'I did it, but I was starving, Sir, and I didn't want to go back to that place.' He looked at the ground. He was uncomfortable, disturbed.

'What place, boy?'

'The place with the stone lion, the place where they hurt you for food.' His broken voice quivered. I don't know if it was the pain of the place he spoke of, or the cold in the room. I raised my brows for him to continue. He ambled towards the door. Leaning on the dirty wall.

'They make me do things, Sir, they make me, preform.'

I didn't want to hear anymore, but I could feel it. Something inside told me to listen, you're worthless unless you just listen.

'I need you to be honest, boy. What did they do there?'

He squirmed like a cornered rat, standing straight. I could feel the shattering cold running through him. I felt it slide up my spine.

'It's not right, Sir, I just want food, Sir, it wasn't my fault.'

His begging triggered the father in me. If I couldn't hear this child, I was useless as a father. I crouched down in front of him, shushing him.

'It's alright, nothing you say can be heard by anyone else,' I whispered to him, just as I would Geoffrey when he was in trouble. 'Trust me, William. I am the only chance you have now.'

Even I glanced down, knowing I wasn't much of a chance myself.

'I—' His lips tightened, a crease in his brow showed a painful memory. 'I'm a good boy, Sir.' He leant towards me, whispering, 'It hurts, sometimes, they put other things in.' I tightened my eyes, knowing where the conversation was going. I didn't want to listen, but I knew I had to. 'Sometimes, it lasts so long, I bleed for days after.'

He stopped talking. As I looked up, I could see the icy grasp of death on him. The boy, at only thirteen years old, held a look I knew well, the look of the condemned man.

They were rare, but sometimes, the gaol offered those upon this Earth a way out, a way to hold their sins for God's forgiveness. He was ready for death, knowing he could escape those who did this to him. There was no other way out for him, and even if there was, he would never be normal again.

'Do you want this, William?' My question tumbled from my mouth as shattered words.

'Billy, Sir, my friends call me Billy, I don't want to die, Sir, but there is nothing else for me here, perhaps God will forgive me, perhaps God will know that I deserve to be forgiven, and perhaps, he will punish those who hurt me.' I slowly stood. I wanted to rip open that cell and march him out myself, but I knew I couldn't. I would find myself on the end of my rope.

'What do you want me to do, Billy?'

He thought for a moment. He didn't have a straightforward answer. He admitted to his crime, but it was barely a crime at all. He could've stolen a cart horse, killed twenty people, and still had the same punishment. His crime was stepping onto the dock on one of Monrow's bad days.

'I would rather like to see my parents again.' His voice was odd, a twisted begging lingered. 'They died a long time ago; I used to visit them often at the Marshes. I remember my mother, but my father, I'm forgetting his face, and I would rather not forget my mother's face. Will they be there, waiting?'

A pain caught my chest, a dulling emptiness fell in my gut. 'Yes, Billy, they'll be there.'

I walked away from his cell. For the first time in ten years, I cried like a newborn babe. Floods of tears drenched my face as I hurried through the forsaken tunnels of Nottingham Gaol. I hid my echoes in the bottom halls of the gaol, the place where the gaolers would gather on a night-time, to await the mournful morrow.

I would never wear a cowardice hood. The condemned deserved to see the face of the man who sent them to their fate. 'Twas something I rather regretted with Billy. The tears I longed to shed for him would have to wait.

The rope tightened. I used the blocks, making sure his neck snapped proper, thick wood tied around his legs and feet, making sure his neck couldn't take his weight. With one last tear, I bid goodbye to Billy, whispering the words I always did.

'Go with God.'

My last saviour was knowing he would never feel the pain of men again. His crime was birth, which is no crime at all.

The night was bitter, leaving the gaol as the screaming gate behind me slammed shut. I never wanted to return to that place, but I knew I had to. For the sake of my family, I needed to kill, so they could live.

The bells followed me home. Our home laid close to the church, 'twas a good wake up call, but haunting, nonetheless.

Her smiling face was there to greet me. I could smell the stew on the boil. Even with the meagre wage I had left she still cooked up a meal. I put my heavy sack on the floor beside the door. A few scraps of meat I'd got from one of the gaolers, whose parents have a farm near town.

'Do you know of a building in town, with a stone lion?' I asked.

She looked up from the table, furrowing her brows towards me. She slowly stepped around.

'I know of a few buildings with stone shapes and statues, but I fail to recall a lion.' Her hands rested on her tiny waist, covered with a pinafore. 'Why?'

I didn't want her knowing the details of my day. It was miserable and so was I.

'Father!' called Bethany, running into the kitchen from the courtyard at the back. She was finally clean, the boy, however, not so clean, he wandered slowly into the kitchen, giving no care for my being there.

'Geoffrey,' called Isabelle, 'greet your father properly.' Her insistence made his head perk up. 'He's had a hard day as it is. Your mood will not help.'

He lifted his eyes towards me. I could feel his resentment, and I couldn't blame him. I resented myself I didn't need him to as well.

'Alright?' he moaned.

I lowered my head.

Isabelle set towards the boy. 'That is exactly what I mean. Sort yourself out, or I'll do it for you!'

I held my hand up to her, 'It's alright, Love, I'll have a word.'

Ambling towards him, I could see he had been playing in the courtyard's pond. The green water tinged his legs. The bottom of his shorts were muddy and wet. The landlord from the Flying Horse had built a small pond where the children could play, 'twas turning out to be a poor idea.

'What is the problem now, boy?'

He glared at me. I knew something had been off for days, but I didn't know how close it was.

'He was my friend, you know, he was just like me, Timmy I mean, he was naughty, but he wasn't that naughty, not enough to get the knot.'

I tried to catch his eyes as he looked down. 'Do you know why I do what I do, son?'

He shook his head. 'It's not really what you do, but how you do it, father.'

The pain in his eyes killed me. He just wanted to understand. I leant close to him. I could see he feared me, but not as a father, as an executioner.

'I need to keep this roof, son, the food in our bellies, that's why, but I suppose you're right. I don't know how. I just have to block it out, to keep you all fed.'

'I would rather starve than lose another Timmy,' his voice broke, he was becoming a man, but it was not a world to grow old in, it was not a world to become a man in, it was a world of suffering.

'I apologise for Timmy, and all those like him.' I came forwards. Taking a stool, I sat in front of him. 'I know there's no comfort now, but before he went, I took him some tuffies from Barker's shop, and I told him he were a good boy, that, what were about to happen, it wasn't his fault, it were the law what failed him.'

He shrugged, brushing it off. 'You are the law, so what are you going to do now?'

I couldn't look at him. 'I don't know, boy, but I will try to do something, I can promise you that.'

They turned in early that night. I thought of my promise, of what I could do, but I thought of Billy more.

he day was a Saturday, I would usually use the day to mull around the gaol, no one would be sent on God's day, and we avoided a weekend hanging, it would draw a bulky crowd, which often showed difficult for the sheriff's men to control.

Since they had suspended the hangings at Gallows Hill, while they carried works out on Mansfield Road, the courtyard had been used for hangings, the public ones were upon the steps, it would always pull a hearty crowd.

I was rather missing my pint of Nottingham Ale from the Nags Head; I would often take the condemned for their last tipple before leading them to their fate.

I wanted to answer Geoffrey's question, and I wanted to answer it honestly. I was a man of God, a devout follower of Christ. Suffering was something I was getting used to, and so I went to the one place where suffering men were welcome.

I would've diverted to the local pub. Instead, I thought of the church on the outskirts of town. A carriage took me, my friend, Robert, he had a farm in the village of

Clifton; he wasn't far from the church, so he offered to take me, I would have to make my own way back, but I knew I could make it back before the midnight hour, if I kept close to the river and followed it towards town.

The bridge over the river wasn't the safest, but the highwaymen stuck to the other side of town. Some of the debtors lived the village, a good friend of mine who would offer the struggling business's a way out of debt keeping them out of my path. Debtors' prisons were some of the worst, filled with poor, dying men and women, where a morsel of bread was a welcome break from the starvation they often faced. Industry crushed the town.

Crunching gravel took me through the heart of the village. The large, picturesque houses reminded me of the small village where I'd grown in Mansfield. The farms and stables were to the far west, despite that, I could smell the freshness, a smell I missed in the dense town. Sweat and filth were a stench we got used to, but when offered something fresh, it made me want to stay.

The light was dull, a large woodland shrouded the village church. I knew of a few churches, but I wished council from someone who did not know my duty upon this earth.

An old winding path took me past the looming graves. Green mosses clung to the headstones; creeping ivy rolled around the trunks of haunting trees. A large, empowering stately home was to the back of the church. I could see the family carriage in the courtyard. I paid no heed to those inside the house and followed the winding path into the church.

The first thing to hit was the fresh smell of old. Churches had a strange smell to me. You can smell the cold air, the bare stone walls, and dusty bibles which lay along each pew. A smell of old wood covered every area of the church.

Echoing footsteps fractured the silence with every step I took. A late hour saw the sun chased from the skies long ago. A few flickering candles lit my way towards the front pew.

'It is rare for someone to venture here at such an hour.' A deep voice echoed, the sound of a man's dull voice. He stepped down the aisle and ambled towards me.

'I apologise.' I stood from the bench, feeling awkward. 'If I inconvenience you, I can return when the time is better.'

'There is no time like the present,' he said with a wide smile across a blush face. Black and white robes covered his large frame. He looked kind, but I was always weary of God's men.

I sat back on the bench, clutching my hands together to pray. I felt the bench shudder as he sat beside me. My eyes were tightly closed, but I could feel his eyes on me.

As I turned my head, I peeked to see him sat silently, his hands clutched together, his eyes closed tightly as he prayed.

'Father, may I ask you something?'

He opened his brown eyes. 'You may ask anything you wish, but please, beware the answer.'

I could tell this would not be a simple conversation.

'Father, is it ever right to kill a man?'

He sat shocked at my question, but society was a strange thing, throw a priest into the mix and it all became so much stranger.

'I suppose what you are asking revolves around the normalities of life, in which case, no, it is not right.'

'And what about abnormal society?'

'Well, in that case, society can be twisted. There are many who deserve the punishment of our Lord and Saviour, but to remove that punishment from the hands of God and deliver it ourselves, is somewhat foolish.'

I felt my brows furrow. 'So, if a man, killed a family, let's say, and his punishment was death by hanging, that would be an unfair punishment?'

'Not unfair. If it is a crime to such degrees we speak of then, I suppose death could at times be the answer.'

I could see he was slightly unnerved; a cold sweat misted his brow.

'I just want to be clear. I have not killed a family of innocents,' I chuckled. He did not. He could see no means for laughter. 'But I have killed, Father, I have taken the lives of so many.'

'And now those lives weigh heavy on your shoulders, as do their crimes.'

I abruptly turned to him; I was desperate. 'How can I live with this?'

My whisper knocked him. 'I assume they deemed those you have killed as guilty for crimes punishable by death, in which case, you are not the one who has killed them, they killed themselves, by acting against God.'

'God,' I sniggered, 'God is not in that place. God would never allow an innocent child to suffer the way I have seen suffering. God would do something—'

'Take the child away, perhaps?' His high tone unravelled his thoughts. 'Death is the only thing in this world we have the right to. The poorest lay with the richest, in the garden of God.'

'So, by killing a child, by hanging a starving child, who had a chance in life, that is showing God's mercy?'

'Who is to say, any child has a chance in life?'

'Who is to say they don't?' His words angered me, but I tried to hold back. 'Many would have a chance, if given one by man, why is everything a decision of God? He gave us free will to prevent such atrocities. Why are we punishing, we should forgive, just as God intended.'

His lips pressed tightly, he smiled from his eyes. 'You sound like a man of God,' he sniggered.

'Why do the men of God allow this?' My voice calmed. I did not want to appear cruel or in any way harmful to him. 'How can an innocent child ever be guilty of the crimes of men?'

He shuffled around on the pew to face me better. A redness in his cheeks shone in the light of the candles.

'My child, you are a man of God, you are a follower of Christ, and as a follower, the message he spread did not end eighteen hundred years ago, it is still alive today, take his message and his word, and do with it what you must, you sound like your decision is made.'

I turned towards him. An anchoring need for help was inside me.

'Can you help me, as a man of God, can you help me save them?'

He slowly stood. 'The church is a sanctuary for all. If someone finds themself within a temple of God, even the law of man, cannot overthrow the laws of God.'

'Keep your doors open, Father. We always need sanctuary in a time as dismal as this.'

'Here.' He turned to the back of him, lifting an unlit lantern. 'Even on the darkest of nights, God's light will shine.'

Taking his answer as a yes. I left the church. The tombstones were barely visible, the night skies darkened the haunting woods. I could hear the river in front, a small signpost on the bottom of a steep muddy hill pointed my way towards town.

I greatly received the lantern, the river towards the banks below was rough and chopping, many had met their end along the banks of the Trent. The silence of the woods remained with me, I had an hour's walk back into town, but by the time I returned, my fate would be sealed, I needed a plan, to end my suffering and the suffering of so many.

Darkness engulfed the road into the horrifying town, drunks being thrown from brothels, faceless women stood along packed street corners, offering their wares, an hour of pleasure was worth the risk to most, but these women were the innocent, forced to the streets by the unstable unfairness of society.

Blocked drains along Gray Friars Gate gave off a stench reaching the entire town. Workers slogged to unblock the foul stench.

Reaching the centre of town, I made my way past the gaol. It was quiet that night, which made an unpleasant change.

Court would be set first thing Monday. Every child deserved a second chance, and I would become that chance.

The house chilled me as I entered, the door, off the latch, was heavy as I pushed it open, my legs ached, the fire went out long ago, but in the corner of the kitchen, lurked a shadow, sat on a small wooden chair.

I took the lantern to light her face. Isabelle had fallen to sleep in the chair. She had never gone to bed without me, and I doubted she ever would. As I looked at her perfect face, I could not help but wonder, how could I, a man of such ill appointment, be so gifted to receive an angel as pure as Isabelle.

Each day she would melt me with her smile. I would have to rise early that morning. I knew she would never rest until we filled our Sunday with words of God.

An early chorus woke me. I took a chair from the table and awkwardly slept beside her, watching her in the dim light of the lantern as she slept. Slowly she woke, removing the blanket I'd put over her.

'What hour is this?' She squinted her puffy eyes.

'We will not miss church, come.' I held my hand out to her. 'The children will be waking soon, and we can start our chaotic morning together.'

'Where were you?'

'I was with God.' Were my words. Her face turned to a pained look. She longed to help me with my vocation, but she knew she could do nothing. 'Worry not, I know what I must do now. Come, Father Donahue frowns upon late comers.'

'Father Donahue is grateful to the few who attend.' She took my hand and stood. Her body ached from the chilly night sleeping on a chair. I could only hope for better nights to come.

Our walk to St Peter's church was welcomed by the bells. A humming from the town that morning woke all. 'Twas a pleasant morning. Dressed to perfection, my small family grew the joyous smile upon my face. I felt normal that day. As we reached the steps to the church, I noticed it, the glares, the whispers, my children could see it, especially Geoffrey.

The delightful morning became a morning of regret. I didn't dislike church, the people turning, peering towards me from over their shoulders. They were the ones who made the morning so regrettable. Upon leaving, I shook the hand of Father Donahue.

'A wonderful sermon, Father, very enlightening.'

'My words are not there to enlighten.' His voice was stripped of humanity, full of the despair of hell. 'They are there to warn, he shall repay good deeds, as he will your sins.'

'Do you believe my duty on this earth to be a sin?'

I felt Isabelle nudge me in the side.

'Your duty is appointed to you by God, George, sins are carried by those who commit such atrocities unto others, you did not commit those, the law is clear.'

'So I may kill a boy of thirteen, because he stole food to quench his hunger?'

'George,' whispered Isabelle.

Father Donahue shuffled, looking at those behind him. 'Well—' he struggled, turning back to me. 'Duty binds you; the law is the law.'

'And if the law calls for a starving child to hang, is my will removed?'

'Well, no, but— yes, I mean, of course you have free will, but the law states what crimes can be punished by death, and you simply follow those laws.'

'Then I am a murderer.' I could still feel her tiny elbow thumping me, trying her best to make me stop. 'My free will has been removed by the laws of man, surely, that would see me as a blasphemer in the least, I should follow the laws of God, but if my duty removes those laws, and I follow the laws of man, what does that make me, Father?'

He calmed, placing a shaking hand on my shoulder he softly said, 'It makes you a man with conscience, a man who is ready to go with God.'

'Do you disagree with the punishment set forth by man, Father?'

He hesitated. 'If God wills it, it shall be done. If God wishes it to end, he will end it.'

I took a heavy sigh; I was hoping for a better answer. 'Then that tells me, the law of man has removed more than my free will, it has also removed the free will of God, he has not stopped it yet, but it needs to end, good day, Father, God bless.'

The walk back was awkward. Isabelle was furious with me, refusing to walk close by my side. Her hat covered her face, red with anger.

'You cannot expect this to continue, Issy.'

She turned sharply, forcing the children to stop. 'I can expect you to hold yourself in the presence of a priest.' She calmed and stepped towards me. She was not one to argue, she always had a need to find a resolve. 'I know it is hard, and I appreciate everything you do, we love you, George, and yes it is hard, the looks, the nods, the constant wagging of tongues, but that is the way of this world, you do what you do to feed your family, to keep them warm and loved.'

Her begging stumped me. I know she loves me, and the children, but I do not love myself, I don't even like myself.

I stepped towards her, taking a knee before her. The children gathered by the side of me. Bethany already had a few spots of mud on her best Sunday dress. Reaching out, I took Isabelle's hand.

'Tell me,' I begged. I did not care for the tears that I felt on my face, although the shocked look from Geoffrey warmed me. He had never seen his father show emotion before. 'I cannot, and I will not, kill another child, another man, guilty of feeding his family, another woman, who has been forced to take, to feed her child, I will not kill another, Isabelle, so please, tell me, what am I to do, when death is the only way to keep us all alive?'

She looked down. She looked at the tears on my cheek, drying them with her gloved hand. 'I can take up work at one of the mills.'

'And me,' Geoffrey spouted, 'they've been asking for children, my size, and Bethany can too. They need small hands and bodies, to crawl along the machines, collecting the fallen wool.'

'I appreciate your thinking, but I would never put you in such danger.'

'Then, why don't we go back?' Isabelle asked.

'But what about the children?' asked Bethany. She stepped forwards, her tiny hand graced my shoulder. 'Daddy needs to be in the bad place, to save the children.'

Her dazzling eyes looked at Isabelle; an idea fell to all of us.

'No, I will not place my family at such risk.'

'But what if we place ourselves there?' asked Geoffrey. 'Why not, Mum? Timmy didn't deserve to die.'

'Timmy, he was different, he was, different.' Her tears flowed. It hurt me to see the pain I caused my family.

I killed that boy, but I never knew his crime. I looked at Geoffrey. 'What happened, Geoff?'

He looked at the floor. A crowd passed by, seeing the hangman on the floor before his wife must have unhinged them, but they passed by with whispers.

'We were playing.' His whimpering voice bothered me. 'It was his turn to hide. It was dark out, so it made it hard for me to try to find him. When I heard it, I ran.'

'Heard what?'

'The man, with a whistle, he blew it, some of the sheriff's men came running, they had Tim by the neck, a bag was over his head, he was hiding in a barrel, he put the bag on his head so I wouldn't see him, they thought he was trying to cover his face so he could steal, it wasn't like that.'

Sickness hit my stomach, knowing that boy was innocent. It was a mistake. But now what? The children were on side. They would help me with whatever I needed to do. Isabelle was a different beast.

'Timmy had no family, he lived at the back of Cow Lane, in a doorway.' His high moaning voice grated at my brain. 'It could've been me, or Beth. They only send them to you to clean the streets, rather than the poorhouses.'

'Isabelle, I know I ask a lot of you, but you've heard that, the boy, Timmy, innocent, the boy, Billy, innocent, he was used as— I can't say in front of the children, but he stole to feed himself, to stay away from hungry men, he was hanged because he was starving, the morrow begins a new week, I cannot see another child to the rope, please, Isabelle, help me, help them.'

Her eyes twisted around the cold cobble stones of St Peters Gate; her mind twisted to our way of thinking.

She was quiet in the kitchen that day. I would allow her time to think. She was much better at planning than I. She had arranged our entire move into town. Not once did I intervene.

A soft sunbeam warmed the cosy drawing room. Quiet muttering from the children on the landing calmed my spirit. I sat on the padded chair reading a small book of poetry.

The words of Lord Byron often spoke so softly to me, I only wished I could one day form something of such beauty for Isabelle. However, I was a simple man, they saved poetry for those of higher classes.

'Alright.' I heard Isabelle forcefully announce. I lowered the book to see her stood at the bottom of the staircase with her hands on her hips. 'I'll do it, but we need a plan, and we cannot do this alone. We need outside help.'

I placed the book on the arm of the chair. 'I have the perfect person in mind, but I need your mind, Issy. I need your mind to do this. I cannot work out how to help them.'

Isabelle returned to the kitchen; I could smell the meat she was cooking that the gaoler had gifted. The meal was almost ready. Bethany and Geoffrey were setting the table.

Slowly, I sat at the head of the table. The children sat silently, waiting for their mother to speak.

'I will need you to tell me everything. We need to do this properly. Every child that is hanged, every innocent man and woman, will walk from that prison, unharmed, if we do this right.'

'Issy, you must understand the danger we face. We can save them, but in turn, we risk the lives of ourselves, and our children.'

She took a deep breath; she had thought the entire day.

'Then the trick is, we don't get caught.' Something she said triggered her, something in her words instantly ignited an idea. 'That's it, we trick them, into believing the guilty party is dead, and then we get them out.' I could feel her excitement.

I started eating. I couldn't hold myself any longer, rumbles from my stomach were becoming embarrassing.

I asked with a full mouth, 'How do you suggest we do that?'

'Where do they take them, after I mean? Who checks that they're dead? I need to know everything.'

I lifted my head. After the first few bites, my appetite withered. 'Well, I suppose that's up to me. I tie, I check, and if needed, I have an assist to help them into the box. From there, I—' I looked at the children; I couldn't speak of such vulgarities in front of them. 'Can we speak of this later, when the children are sleeping—'

'We need to know, Dad,' Geoffrey pestered.

I looked at him from the corner of my eye. Bethany looked frightened. She was three years younger than he, and her ears were not made for such ugly talk.

'When your sister's in bed.'

'Well, I may have a plan, but this will take outside help.' Isabelle looked at Bethany; she too could see the look of worry on her tiny face. 'Don't worry, darling, eat your dinner and then to bed.'

Bethany was not a child to argue. She was a good girl. Like her mother, she would look to God for answers, but God had answered all our questions. My family was willing to work towards God's will, although he spoke no words to me. What I had seen were the actions of man. God had spoken to me through them.

'This will be God's work,' I softly whispered to Isabelle.

She reached over the table, placing her hand on my forearm. 'Of course it will, Love, God will work through us, as a family.'

With Bethany in bed, the house became quiet. We gathered at the table, the church lantern lit on our faces, I sat with Isabelle and Geoffrey, ready to deliver them to my world of atrocities. Bethany had been asleep for over an hour. I felt safe to talk.

'We're hanging at the gaol now. The works along Mansfield Road hinder our route. Before they are taken, I check my papers, to see what order I have, I visit them in their cells—'

'Alone?' Isabelle jumped.

I nodded. 'I tell them what they are to do. Upon receiving their sentence, I place the rope around their neck, and I hang them. Sometimes, I have an assist, to help with other duties. If the sentence is on the step, we must carry them back inside, whereupon they are searched for belongings, most of the time they will have a few coins, it's a hangman's tip, they're stripped of their clothes, some executioners take them home, but I take them to the poorhouses and workhouses instead.' I could feel the shame in my voice. Every word I spoke killed me a little more inside.

'It's alright, Dad, keep going.' I looked at Geoffrey. He was no longer a child. He was a man now, showing so much strength in the light of his father's duty.

'From there, the body is taken to the cold room, it's put into a box. Sometimes, I get requests, from doctors, who wish to buy the corpse, for experiments.' Isabelle winced, sitting back, a look of disgust was plastered on her face. I was further ashamed of myself. 'I only ever send the real murderers and scum, that's how we afforded the last mass, I had two in just as many days, anyway, from there they are taken to the cemetery and buried, their last rites are often miserable, I attend myself, as often as I can, knowing the shame they brought to their family often keeps them away.'

'So, no family, no friends, nothing?' asked Geoffrey. I could see the sadness greying his face. It hurts me as a father, and it hurts me as a man.

'No, son, they are kept until the morrow, then taken to the church, and given a burial.'

'Are you there, all the way through?' asked Isabelle, her fascination turned to obsession.

'As soon as that last nail is in, I'm done, what I choose to do is not my duty, however, if I wished, I would not even see them to the cart, my assist is the one to take them to the marsh. Once they're all lined up, they'll be carted off from there.'

'So, who checks them?'

'Well, we did have a physician on site, but since his wife passed, he hasn't been turning in, so I do that—' I lifted my eyes to her. She already had a plan, she was just securing everything. I knew how her beautiful mind worked.

Her smile grew as her eyes relaxed. 'Geoffrey, to bed with you, we have work to do.' Isabelle told him, but her eyes remained on me.

'I can do this, George, we can do this, we can create life after death, but only for the innocent, to take their place, will be the guilty, the truly guilty.'

She was a worker once. The mills were working fast, spinning new lace and threads, but no one was faster with a needle than Isabelle. Her time in the mills ended when the new machines were introduced. Industry was taking over, taking the jobs from the workers. The women were the first to go. She had never involved herself with the vulgarities of the riots, instead she remained as any lady should, lending her hand to the church, being a good neighbour, with our plan in mind, she would become the best neighbour anyone could ever hope for upon the dull and dismal streets of Nottingham.

I'm a farmer's boy, she is from a wealthy enough house, her father took a liking to me early on, he saw promise in me, so did her mother, Anna, I was yet to see that promise in myself, but as the night lingered, and as Isabelle worked, I was slowly starting to see that promise, blossoming from my astonishing wife.

Chapter Three God's Plan

he weather was typical for that time of year, chilly rain ran down the gutters of Cow Lane. A stench of muddy filth ran drifted in from the river Leen on the far side of town.

Our home sat towards the back of Peck Lane, 'twas a pleasant street, usually quiet, apart from the pub on the corner, where ne'er-do-wells would spill into the street at ungodly hours, singing of their misery in the echoing, tightly packed streets.

Isabelle knew the neighbours well; our Geoff had many young friends with the neighbours. A lot of the friendships were forced by parents, scared of their neighbour, the hangman, the killer. Being friends with the executioner's son, triggered a certain loyalty with them, believing I would spare them where their fate to change. Little did they know I had no say over anything.

Works at the bottom of Low Pavement blocked the road. I often wandered along different streets upon my going to and coming from the gaol. Keeping my head in the crowd was the duty of the town executioner. I was their warning. A strong view for any who disobeyed the law.

'Morning, George.' Came a voice from behind me, void of emotion, I know exactly who that voice belongs to.

A sweat covered brow in the middle of winter, and a strong fragrance of beer wafted from his overcoat.

'Morning, Percy.' I tipped my hat, I'm far from rude, always wearing a mask to cover the misery within.

I took the long way around. I felt his eyes on me as avoided the market of Weekday Cross. Instead of the busy crowds, I headed towards Swine Green, turning onto Stony Street.

The gaol was quiet. I feared what the court had planned. I prayed for no more children.

The hour was early, the new whale oil lanterns lining the streets were slowly dulling, having spent the night burning their oil off. A bitterness hit me, but it was refreshing, knowing that I had a week of gaoler duties before the hangman would again be needed.

My place in the gaol saw me in a privileged position.

'Good morning again, George,' greeted Percy stood on the steps.

I made my way in. He was an odd soul, small of stature, not usual for a gaoler.

'Percy, what duties have you today?'

He sighed, looking at the misery of the weather behind me. 'Chief has me on the Weekday, swine day, lucky me.'

'Ah, you'll need it. I avoided it this morning for that very reason. I can already hear them.'

The day would see me comfortable in the court, seeing the lawbreakers coming and going, waiting to see that one man, woman, or child in need of my wife, and her stunningly crafted saviour.

Settling on the benches had me at a perfect angle to see the innocent and guilty. I would be the judge now. The useless Judge Frank Monrow ambled his way into the court. He hated being called Frank.

The first on the dock was a drunk, much like the judge, who would now decide his fate. The man stank of ale, filth, and vomit. Plucked from the gutter for public disorder, as his first offence the judge was lenient with him, five years in the hellish gaol.

The second in was equally as boring. They charged him with the rape of a young girl. The evidence was overwhelming. Given that his own father caught him in the act, I would take great pleasure in seeing him upon my rope. Sentenced, instead, to transport to a foreign land, rewarded for his crimes in my eyes.

The day lingered, ne'er-do-wells and disturbers were all that graced the room that morning, but as the afternoon lingered, my eyes sank. Tiredness took hold. I folded my arms, hoping judge Monrow would not catch me sleeping.

'No, Sir,' I heard the small voice call from the dock. A crowd gathered to see this one in. 'I brushed past the man in the street. I took nothing, Sir, I have no need to.'

The rumbling voice of Frank replied, 'You have no need to?'

'No, Sir, I took up work in the mill, Sir, last year, it doesn't pay great but it's enough for food and warmth, the foreman is kind, it keeps me from the workhouses—'

'Yes, I've heard this before.' His wide blue eyes scared the young boy in the dock. He looked no older than thirteen.

'So, your wage feeds you, clothes you, and keeps you sheltered, even in winter months?'

'Yes, Sir, in the winter, the foreman, he lets me sleep in the mill, keeps the burglars out, if someone's in there, he doesn't have to pay for someone else to do it, and I get a warm sleep.'

Monrow nodded. The prosecution stood, ready to question the shivering wreck upon the stand which engulfed the child.

'So, you claim you brushed past him, however, upon inspection, they found his coin purse on the ground close to your feet when you were caught by the police.'

'Well... he may have dropped it?' The boy panicked. I sat forward, secretly, I was hoping for it, needing them to say it, begging for the bastard of a judge to sentence the poor creature to hang.

The trial lasted only a few minutes. The judge turned to the jury beside him, two men of higher society. Monrow nodded at a man on the right of him.

Slowly, the fat man stood. He held a sneering look of disgust as he looked at the boy.

'Guilty, my lord.'

'Yes!' I silently whispered.

The boy screamed. Terror on his face told me he knew his fate. I could hardly hear Monrow over the boys screams and cries of innocence.

'As the law of our land states, pick-pocketers, ne'er-do-wells, rogues and vagrants are not welcome among our society. You have shown the court here your contempt, you have lied to us all, you are a criminal, and at such a young age, there is no fixing such crooked mistakes of nature. Andrew Marcus Biggins, you will be hanged by the neck until dead, may God have mercy on your soul.'

Oh, he will, he will have mercy on his soul. I trust Isabelle, and I know she will save that young boy. Her hands will see him to freedom, and I will be there to make sure of it.

The gaol appeared brighter that day, sun-drenched halls guided me through the corridors, dust swirled and danced in the enchanting beams. I stepped into the children's wing; I had never felt a feeling as light as this one. We planned to evict Andrew from purgatory, he would be free from his sin, and he would see a chance at life again.

I had to compose myself, a heavy feeling of excitement churned my gut, I knew he would be saved, and I knew his excitement would need to be calmed. He was a good boy, just like Billy, only Andrew would live to see many more days to come.

The cold stone walls warmed, I could hear the sobbing from the end cell, children's faces glared towards me from their cells, they were somewhat lucky, having been sent to the gaol by parents and guardians, to instil some discipline, they were not there for crimes as such, they would walk freely from the gaol, as reformed inmates.

The sobbing died as I approached his cell.

'To your work, boy,' I ordered. I feared being caught by a gaoler. I was to deliver the boy some stunning news, but I needed to be sure they would not hear us.

'What is the point, Sir, I am to die, to be hanged by the neck until dead. Words are no use now. Writing on parchment isn't going to save my life, Sir.'

I looked at the corridors; the boy scrunched in the corner of his cell.

'Come here, boy.' I tried to use a soft approach. He looked like a cornered dog. I needed him closer.

He shuffled his way towards the door. He struggled to stand. Grief took his strength.

'Where are your parents?'

'Died, Sir, a fever took them.'

'And how old were you?'

'I was nine when they went, Sir, it was a pauper's burial, at the Marshes, but I'm not ashamed of that, I've survived since, by God's honesty, I did not touch that man's coin purse.'

'Alright, I need you to lower your voice.' I could hear the echoes up the corridor. I knew the other children would hear. 'You aren't set for a week yet, I'm the only executioner of the gaol.' His face changed. He thought I was a gaoler, but floods of tears fell from his face upon realising my vocation.

'I won't see you on my rope, Andrew. We will get you good and clear of this place. All I need you to do, is listen, and do everything I tell you to do.'

I showed that boy more than he should know. He had never been to a public hanging before, even though children as young as nine would usually attend with their parents. I had to show him everything, how his face would look, what his legs would do, how long it would last, a boy of his frame would take a good few minutes, he would need to act, and act well.

My return home was met with a better greeting, only Isabelle remained silent by the fire in the kitchen. Upon her lap, there it sat, her final plan. She stood with the garment held high for me to see. A thin jacket, but it was so much more than that. It was a life jacket.

I held it; I felt the craft of her hands in my fingers.

'It contains within, twenty ropes, which all lead toward a central rope up the spine.' She showed me the brilliance with her delicate fingers.

'It will fit them like a jacket, under their clothes, the leg straps stop it pulling up, I added a few buckles to size them properly, of course I will have to make an adult one, but here.' She showed me the top of the jacket, where the central rope from the spine contained a silver hook. 'You attach the other rope to this. It will hide in the neck of the noose, so it will look like they're hanging, but all that will hang is the jacket.'

My laughter lit her face. Something happened that day, something I had not felt in all too long. The corners of my mouth curled upwards, a smile formed, my mouth opened as I laughed with joy.

'This is brilliant, Issy.' I lifted her from the ground, celebrating her accomplishment. 'I knew you could do this.'

From the back courtyard, the children came with their excitement.

'Before we do this, we need to test it,' said Isabelle, widening her eyes with excitement.

'Who can we test it on?'

'Me!' called Geoffrey. He stepped towards me, adamantly.

'Geoff, this is still dangerous.' I panicked. I didn't wish to hang a child. I certainly didn't wish to hang my own.

'Do you trust mother?' asked Geoffrey.

'Of course I do, but this is different—'

'No, it's not.' His argument was valid, and I struggled to argue back. 'Father, get a noose.'

'Twas a macabre activity. Hanging children within my house should never have been such fun, but to Geoffrey and Isabelle, well, I had never heard them laugh so hard. I remained back, learning the best way to use her skilled jacket.

A wooden beam which ran across the house, separating the kitchen from the upstairs, would act as the perfect beam. It was like the one I used, only indoors.

Throwing the rope over, I felt ill, seeing Geoffrey wearing the jacket under his clothes. It worried me they would see it, but it was perfect. He placed the noose around his neck, constantly wearing a smile.

Stood on a chair, he took pleasure in the macabre act of hanging. Isabelle wore a wide grin as she stepped towards Geoffrey.

'Geoffrey Roderick Smith, for crimes of being far too handsome, you are to hang by the neck until you are dead.'

She lifted her leg and kicked the chair from beneath him. I failed to react quick enough. Jumping forwards, I held him to the rafter.

'Let him go,' she laughed. My heart beat from my chest, failing to see the amusement.

'Dad, I'm fine, let me go.'

I stepped back, slowly letting him down. The noose tightened, but just enough to redden his face, and not enough to snap his neck.

'Do it, Geoff.' I saw the need in her bright eyes.

He flailed his legs, kicking and choking. Luckily, Bethany would be collected later from her lessons at the church. That boy was a marvel. I could see the icy grasp of death in his eyes, but his life was fully inside of him still. This truly was God's work.

'Shall we let him down?' asked Isabelle. Stepping to the side of me, she rested her head on the side of my chest. 'This really can be done.'

'We could leave him up there?' I sniggered.

'George Smith,' she gasped as she stood straight. 'Did you just make a joke?'

'Comedy isn't my strong point, I know.'

The boy continued to flail in the back, proving the device worked.

'It has been far too long, but brighter days are ahead now, not only will we save the innocent, but we will also save Nottingham.'

She stepped towards him, untying the noose. She quickly unclipped the rope. Geoffrey remained in character. Playing dead was something he was stunningly good at.

'This is brilliant, Issy.' I could not contain my excitement at her success.

Geoffrey opened a single eye. 'Now all you need to do, is make sure anyone using it knows what they're doing.'

'Well, I was going to talk to you about that.' I looked at Geoff, he was of age, only ten years old, but an assist could start from the age of nine. 'John, my assist, he has joined Connor Ashworth, in Lincoln, so, this could be your chance as an assist.'

'No,' Isabelle pelted forwards. 'I see your thinking, George, but he is only ten. He will still run the risk of seeing actual hangings.'

She was right. I could not allow him to be further tainted by his father.

'Very well, so, we need to find a new assist, someone who we can trust, someone who isn't afraid of such an undertaking.'

'I can think of no one,' she said with a heart fluttering sigh. 'Oh, George, we cannot come all this way for it to fail. We need to find someone, fast.'

'Well, I have a boy, Andrew. I've got a few before him, but they are set for Monday. We will need someone before then.'

I had set us a new task, to find someone we could trust would not be easy in the cold town, full of drunken scum, many would give their right arm to see the death of the hangman, and their left to take my place at the rope.

Isabelle was different, a friend of all. Her place in the town saw her constantly busy. She would feed the poor when needed, clothe the needy, and place herself at the forefront of all matters of importance.

A dull morning greeted me, making my way through the town. A distinct carriage passed by as I walked through Smithy Row. The black carriage was one I oddly recognised. The rear wheels had clearly seen the carriage along the lanes towards Derby, the empty roads were sure to keep it clear of mud and debris. I paid little more heed to the carriage and continued my way towards the gaol.

The early dawn brought a fresh dew from the surrounding farms, the town was pleasant that morning, a flurry of workers, for the new systems of sewer works, were arriving at the town early to start their work, it was noisy, but it drowned out the calling from inside the gaol.

The looming walls looked cold that day. My mission was still at hand, I took my place among the gaolers and made my way towards the court.

Three people would meet their fate that day. A drunk would serve only six years for an evening of merrymaking. A young woman accused of partaking in drunken behaviour would spend the next ten years of her life inside an asylum. Francis saw her act as lewd and unbecoming of a young lady. They were husband and wife, celebrating their new lives together, his lesser sentence spoke of the unfairness women often faced.

The last man to stand that day intrigued me. Adrian Eccles, his crime was little more than a brawl outside a local brothel, however, Francis clearly disliked Adrian. A twenty-year sentence was unjust. There was nothing I could do for these poor souls. At least they would have their lives at the end of their service.

I took my place beside the bench of Judge Monrow. Waiting for the court to clear, I knew he would have specific orders for me; he liked a comfortable rope.

Stepping into his chambers behind him, he began to de-robe, passing his robes to me to hang up for him as he did.

'I know next week will be a busy one for you, George, with three on the roster already, and still only a Tuesday. If this goes on, we shall have to add another day.' His chuckling laugh grated at me; I hated the man.

'Yes,' — I gave a forced smile, — 'although, the young boy, he could be placed back a week if needed.'

'Poppycock,' he chalked, 'that boy is nart but a ne'er-do-well, a waste in today's society, I have told you before, George, we are building a better world, by removing the warts from the face of decent society.'

I could feel my blood boiling, my heart raced, and I struggled to calm it. His society he spoke of had no place for men like me, those who cared for the life of a fellow man.

'I can only agree, my lord,' my response wavered.

'Please, George.' He turned towards me, unbuttoning his tight shirt from the top of his neck. I knew the size of rope I would need for that one. 'I have told you before, you are my town executioner. Call me Francis. We are colleagues, and everyone wishes to be friends with the hangman.' His grin pained me. Seeing that smug look drowned from his face would be the only thing that would bring me pleasure.

'Very well, Francis, but as I say, you know the hangings of children often call a crowd to the steps, the last time it took several of the sheriff's men to disperse them, this time, we may not be so lucky. A private hanging may be better placed on this occasion.'

'Is the boy known?'

I knew where he was going with this.

'No, Sir, I mean, Francis, he is known in the mills though, that could be enough to begin another knitter's riot. The last thing we need during such austerity is for the Luddites to start again, they seek any excuse.'

He boomed towards me. 'Therefore, I like you, George, you have a way with people, you're quiet, yet you're placed, you know where you belong, and with that, I agree, another riot in the town would cause unrest among friends.'

That was all he cared about, what others thought of him, what table he would dine at. I cared nothing for my table, so long as my family were with me.

A private execution would ease our plan for Andrew. I was yet to find another who could join my side. With less than a week before his fate was sealed, I needed to find my assist.

Returning home, the bells above St Peters threw their deep sound, bouncing up alleyways, towards the large market and beyond, meeting the bells of St Mary's. The busy streets died, the pubs remained quiet, the law was out that night, seeing some of the local police and watchmen walking through the streets brought comfort to some, to others it brought heart-stopping terror and dread.

'Evening, George,' greeted Godfrey. He was a large man. The grey-faced police officer had gained his title through bribery and greed.

'Godfrey.' I gave a small nod, showing some manners. 'You'll have me busy for the next few weeks I hope.'

'At this rate we'll be keeping you busy until the next mass, three tonight already, and a new investigation, a woman reported a rape last evening, we shall be investigating on the morrow.'

'Well, I can only pray you catch the culprit. The more villains off these streets, the better.'

'Quite, evening to you, George, send my regards to Isabelle.' His smarmy face was ripe for a beating.

'Of course, she always mentions when she passes the law of the streets.'

'I only hope we make her feel safe.'

'Yes.' I gave a grin. I tried to smile but my face wouldn't let me. 'Good evening, Godfrey, gentlemen,' I said as I nodded at the few officers surrounding him.

My pace quickened up Stony Street and towards Swine Green. I could not wait to see Isabelle that evening. The children would be a delight for me to see. I needed my family for the sake of my sanity, were it not for them, I would've seen the asylum long ago.

Stepping inside, the heat from the fire hit me, our coal would usually be saved for visitors, I knew someone was there, what I didn't expect was the cold glare from my father-in-law sat at the rusty brown table, his eyes pierced me.

'What a pleasure,' I gleefully rejoiced as I stepped inside, placing my cloak on the hook at the side, I hurried in. 'To what do we owe such pleasure?'

Isabelle was in the kitchen. She slowly turned, a face filled with tears met me. Rushing towards her, Roderick didn't move. He remained with his hands wrapped around his cup.

'What is it?' I asked as I held her close.

'Mother, she passed a week ago, we've received nothing. I didn't get a chance to say goodbye.'

Her whimpers were cruel. I had taken her away from her final days with her parents, only to spend her days in a rat-infested hellhole.

'He knows,' she whispered.

I turned to Roderick. His eyes remained with the cup in his hands, a glum look of loss on his face spoke of the love he had for Anna.

'My deepest apologies, Father, I did not know, and I certainly would have been there if I did.'

'I know.' His voice was a broken whisper of loss. I knew how he felt, but a fraction of the thought of losing Isabelle hit me, churning my gut.

'You're one of the good ones, George. Isabelle has told me your duty in this town.'

I sank back into my pit of despair, not wanting him to continue.

'Honestly, what you do takes heart. It takes a man to end a man, but a child, George.' His sighing voice concerned me; disappointment filled him. 'Why did you not tell me sooner?'

'Village affairs are far different from a town, especially one which grows as rapidly as this one. I never wanted to do what I came to do, but the wage, it keeps me, and the family, it allows for me to pay for my mistakes, and keep your daughter in good standing.'

'And you believe a career such as this is safe? Revenge is an ugly beast. The children are not safe while you continue such things.' He sat back in his chair, looking at me with shame. 'I know you made mistakes, George, but such blatant callousness is not like you.'

'It was either this or the watchmen. Even the police get half the wage I do, and they all keep an eye on the house. They keep a close watch on the children—'

'That is what concerns me, Derby is far, but we do receive the press papers, they tell us of hangings and other such nasties of the town, now I know, my son-in-law, who is more of a son to me than my own, is responsible for such horrors.'

'I feel shame enough. I have spent nights and days hating myself. I do not need you to hate me, too. I hate the man I am.'

Isabelle walked towards me, putting her hands on my shoulders.

'I do what I do for this family, to keep us above the scum of lower society, but I do not want to be a part of their society, they see me only as the hangman, each day I leave this house, I have to act my way through the day, doing my best not to break down and scream in that court.'

He lowered his head. 'She has also told me of your plan.' He looked into my eyes; I could sense so much more from him. 'Anna, she was my life, my everything, I came here today, because the farm has been sold, I was looking for property in town, and perhaps a new vocation, as an assist should see fit.'

I belted forwards, panicked. 'You know the risk involved?'

He leant back in his chair. 'It was a risk you would willingly place my daughter in. I would rather take her place. As an assist to my son-in-law, our secret remains with us. You also neglect to realise I am connected.'

'I know, that was why I visited him.'

Isabelle stepped back, unsure about who I spoke of.

'He said he would help, when we get these people out, they are to be taken to the church in the village of Clifton, the priest has offered sanctuary, from there, it will be their choice, a second chance to go with God.'

'That is, if God welcomes them.' Roderick was doubtful of our plan, but the old man simply wanted a second chance to do right by his daughter.

Roderick was an honest man. He began life as a hardworking farm hand, turning his skills to engineering. He now ran several mills in the village of Derby. The large farm where he grew would fetch a good price.

We were God's family now, and as Andrew's day drew closer, we felt unprepared, but looking back, we were better prepared than we needed to be.

I did not creep down the corridor of the children's wing. The gaol was noisy that day, filled with the moans and groans of villains awaiting their fate. A confident walk took me towards his cell. A gaoler at his cell had me slightly unnerved.

'A moment alone with my prisoner please, Raymond.'

'Certainly, George, today is a big day for this one, go easy on him,' said Raymond, he was just like the other gaolers. They felt pity for the children in that cell, knowing their fate was often undeserved.

'Don't worry, this will be quick, and fair.'

Raymond walked away, looking into the different cells as he left.

'Good to see you, George.'

'And you, Andrew, quickly, come here,' I whispered at him. Andrew was a good student. I had made a visit with him each day, teaching him the proper way to die. Pressing the jacket through the bars, I whispered, 'Take your shirt off and put this on, quickly.'

He hurriedly did exactly as I asked. I only prayed they would all be so easy. Andrew would be the first of God's children, but he would not be the last.

He pressed his face on the door. 'George,' he whispered. I crouched down to hear him better. 'I'm scared.'

'I know. Keep crying, Andrew, it will help your case, just remember, by the morrow, you will be well on your way to the true house of God, go with God, Andrew, there you will have a second chance.'

The gaoler's quarters were empty, a single small box lay on a table, the courtyard through a large red door was empty, a couple of gaolers wandered there. Roderick remained by the side of the box coffin.

His eyes stared at the common light wood.

'I know,' I whispered at him, knowing the sight disturbed him. 'Remain with a face on this, Roderick, none of this is real, remember that, just look horrified, but not too horrified, you need to remain as my assist, any shows of weakness will see you from these walls, I have seen gaolers removed for less.'

'I don't know how you do it, George—'

'To feed my family, to keep your daughter safe. Now, God's work awaits us. Andrew will be here soon. First, we have a criminal to hang.' He turned to see a larger box laid out on the floor. 'This will be a real hanging; you know what to do?'

He nodded. I knew I would need to trust him. Keeping everything within the family would see our chances of survival grow.

'John Muller, you have been found guilty of the crime of murder, you are to hang by the neck until you are dead.'

A shudder ran up Roderick's spine, I could see it as I spoke those words.

The sound of the falling stool always echoed through the courtyard. He struggled on the rope, I leant forwards and whispered, 'Go with God, John. He awaits you.'

I was shocked at Roderick's behaviour. He remained plain face. It was a fast and efficient death. Roderick helped lift him, giving no care to the bodily fluids which had already begun oozing from the unfortunate. Lumping him into the box, I checked John was dead before the lid was placed onto the top and the nails driven in.

I gave Roderick a look of pride, but as I did, I saw Andrew over his shoulder, being forcefully led in by one of the gaolers. As soon as the boy saw me, he relaxed.

'Are you ready for this, Andrew?'

'I will never be ready, Sir, but as you say, God is ready for me, so I must go with God.'

The gaoler clinging to his shirt raised his brows, impressed. I had calmed Andrew. I had a way with children, but my gift of calming them should never have been used to lead them peacefully towards their death.

'Are you ready for this?' I asked Roderick.

'As I'll ever be.'

Taking him out to the yard was painful and perfect. The noose around his neck fitted beautifully. I had the perfect measurements. I knew the boy would do well. As the stool dropped, Roderick squinted, Andrew kicked his legs, I could see his face turning red and puffy, the flailing rope looked tight, his tied hands clutched, an entire three minutes of struggling was the best act I had ever seen, he was fighting for his life.

His legs stopped kicking, limp and lifeless, his body swayed in the light breeze, his eyes were slightly open, his face was still red but formed a blue tinge, perfection at its best.

We untied the noose, unclipping the rope as we did. I placed him in the small box; I heard a rustle as we drove the nails into the coffin.

Leaning down, I whispered, 'A few more hours, Andrew, we'll see you away. Knock once if you hear me.'

It was like waiting for the dawn on a long winter night. Finally, he gave a faint knock.

Roderick nodded at me, noticing a shadow approach from the hall behind us.

'That went well,' said Francis passing into the room, he would usually avoid that area of the gaol. It haunted him, knowing he had sent many there, most of which were innocent.

'Yes, Francis, I believe there are few who will struggle on my rope.' I tried to mock, but it was not a place for mockery. I simply followed the rules laid down by many before me.

'I am yet to meet your father-in-law.' He held a hand to Roderick, who, being a man of good repute, took the judge's hand for a hearty shake.

'I hear good things, your honour.' Roderick attempted pleasant conversation. Over the body of a child was not the place for anything pleasant.

'And yet I am yet to hear anything myself,' joked Francis, 'unfortunately, I have little time within this place, my court constantly fills with the gutter of this town.'

'Rats, your honour, but all we can do is clear one at a time. Given time, the others will learn to heel, they will learn to become decent people among society. Most importantly, they will learn their place within it.'

Francis was not a man to show emotion, but he liked Roderick, I could tell, the snivelling words Roderick spoke were exactly what Francis longed to hear from any hangman's assist.

'I can with honesty say I like you.' He looked at the wooden box, covered with a white sheet ready to be carted to the Marshes Burial Ground. 'May I ask, what was your vocation before choosing this fine town?'

'I was an engineer, Sir,' replied Roderick, 'nothing of substantial importance, but I chose the life of the town, to see my autumn days with my grandchildren.'

'You're far too modest.' I stepped towards Roderick. While untying a rope, he often saw his achievements as meagre. 'This man was responsible for new works along the Leen. Were it not for him, the water would've remained brown in the town.'

Francis widened his impressed eyes, 'Well, that is certainly an achievement.'

'It is, but the growth of the town will soon see my work as obsolete, the town is growing, the Leen can only handle so much, eventually, they will need a much larger works than the one I put in place, a much larger company will soon take on the town, in fact, any good man of strong mind would see fit to invest in the next water company along these banks, including the Trent.'

Pinched lips and a downward smile showed on Francis's face. He was overly impressed with my talkative father-in-law.

'Then I shall do just that. Inside information is something I will always welcome.'

'He only helps me here because there are few I would trust with your ropes, Francis,' I quickly interjected.

'Well, of course I don't need to be here, such vulgarities are usually saved for younger men, but George would simply trust the law to no other, he requires a very specific duty of an assist, and it is a duty I will willingly provide, to clean these streets of the detritus which currently befalls it.'

I could see Francis brimming with glee. He would usually save such excitement when sentencing a rapist or mugger, murderer, or common thief.

'I would be most pleased to see you at my table this year. Our barley feast will come after spring. I shall see you before then and be sure to send you an invitation.'

'And it would honour me to accept it.' Roderick was good, better than I thought he would be, or even could be.

Our way back that night saw us with shaking hands, an uncomfortable feeling in the pits of our stomachs churned. We would need to rise early, to see the boy out before the dawn.

'Who buries them?' asked Roderick, making our way back through High Pavement and towards Fletcher Gate.

'The gravediggers.' I planned on taking Roderick to the Flying Horse at the end of the housing row.

'Are we to exhume the boy's grave? Surely he will die before then?'

'Certainly not,' I whispered. I knew the watchmen were on duty that evening, given the quietness of the town. 'When we arrive on the morrow, they load the bodies onto carts, it is the duty of my assist to take them to the Marshes—' I stopped walking and turned. 'Surely Isabelle has told you this?'

Shaking his head, his aging cheeks jiggled.

'When leaving the yard, make your way through High Pavement, the judge insists that the town sees the coffins of the deceased, as a warning to lawbreakers, from High Pavement follow the road to Middle Pavement and onto Low Pavement, Isabelle will be waiting for you in a small alleyway, Pepper Lane, a building there is empty, following the riots, she will take the boy's coffin, and replace with a weighted coffin, carry on your way and the diggers will deal with the rest. On the way back, go through the lane, Isabelle will take it from there.'

'She told me none of this.' He was frightened, his act was depleting.

'I am sure she would've, but we need an early rise. Come, we need to get home, before the watch arrives.'

We practiced our plan, everything went perfectly, Andrew remained silent. He was the first we saved. We only wished the others would be as good as he was.

Seeing Andrew in the arms of the priest at the church of Clifton made my heart swell. He would remain in the church with the priest, helping where he could, and hiding when he had to. Andrew was dead. The law would never come looking for him. The family of God felt its first victory.

Chapter Four God's Will

My days in the gaol became weighted. A heavy feeling remained with me. The children's wing brought a different feeling now, where the ghosts of children would linger. They faded; a welcome hum lingered where once there were a cold and bitter foreboding. Having saved more than five already. Forgiveness from the ghosts was detectable.

The summer was pleasing that year, they had planted new flowers in the yard of St Mary's, a freshness hit the town and drowned the gaol. Our plan had worked for children, but God's will would reach further than children alone.

The court was dusty and dry, a mid-afternoon beam flooded through the upper windows, it clearly bothered Frank, who kept squinting his eyes towards the dock, a heavy mood had caught his heavy head, having spent the night drinking with his highbrow friends and acquaintances.

A small woman made her way into the dock. It was a grim day for her; she had caught Monrow at a time of the day when lunch was calling. His hanging head wanted a quick resolve to her crime.

'Annabelle Hawkins.' She struggled to say her name. She was a pretty little thing. Her dirt filled fingernails clearly bothered her. She tried to pick the dirt from under them without the judge and jury seeing.

'Annabelle Hawkins.' Frank leant forwards, clutching his forehead in his hand. 'I see here you are charged with the grotesque murder of a client.' He looked at her with raised brows, trying to look down on her further.

She whiffled her head. The prosecution stood, to ask her the most despicable of questions.

'Annabelle, walk us through the night's events.'

'Well, Sir, I was at the Back Side, about to turn down Broad Lane, I felt something pulling on me, as I turned a figure behind me pushed me to the ground, he took me, Sir, I ain't no bad un, I ain't never seen a man before, not like that, and when the watchmen came, I told em, I said what 'appened, but all tha' worried them, were the blood, I pushed the man off, he fell back, hitting his head on a stone wall on the Lane before the law got there, I didn't mean to, I just wanted him off me.'

Her begging eyes fuelled me. I knew her face. She sold orchard apples on the Market at Weekday Cross, she was no woman of the evening, she was an honest woman, who had befallen a terrible fate.

'In light of events, would you say his injuries were worse than yours?' asked the snarling prosecution.

'The man, he's dead, so yes, but I didn't—'

'There we have it, your honour, a man, who was simply out for business. Perhaps he didn't pay you enough?' he asked her. She looked horrified. Before she could answer, he went on, 'Perhaps, you were expecting more, or planning to rob him? We have seen an increase in such crimes. The man did not deserve to die but still he did. You acted as judge, jury and executioner. You killed him because he would not pay you enough—'

'I am not a whore!' her voice deepened; her hands shook. 'I am an honest woman.'

'Unmarried, at the age of—' He looked at his sheets—'twenty-four, and still unwed.' His eyes drifted to the jury. 'I can see where this is going, an unwed woman of that age, she is tainted, wanted by no man and so she sets about robbing and killing.' He slammed back into his chair.

'I 'ain't married, I took over my father's business when he died, at the orchard. Some men, they wanted to buy it, but I said no—'

Her panic was instantly shut down, the foreman stood. 'Guilty, your honour.'

'I did nothing but defend myself,' she squealed like a stuck pig.

I heard her being led from the dock, unable to hold her squeals of innocence. God's will has changed, it would now include women.

The adult part of the gaol was different. It was noisy; they were not given tasks to complete along the wing of the condemned. Men and women were mixed. Rape was more prevalent in the gaol than it was on the streets.

The stench was different. A bodily odour kept many of the gaolers away from the wings. The air was filled with the moans and groans of insane men and women who would probably fare better within the asylums. An area of the condemned brought a different smell, a smell of fear was thick in the air, a sound of dripping water from a leak in an unkempt roof, the odd few sounds of rattling chains from the more uncooperative of offenders.

The sound that hit me as I walked through the wing, was one I would never forget, I could hear her shivering. A cold summer hit the gaol that evening. I was ready to leave the gaol, but I could not leave her thinking herself dead already.

Silently she sat, her face drenched with silent tears. Her head was shaking back and forth, as though she was begging with nothing, telling it, she did nothing wrong.

Her eyes drifted towards me, the darkness in the wing drowned out my features. A lantern behind me must have terrified her. She said not a single word, she simply stared at me, giving the sweetest smile. The small girl reminded me of the innocence of Isabelle.

'Worry not, Annabelle, I know what you are, I shall see you on the morrow.' Her eyes gave an ice-cold glare. The poor thing was petrified of everything in her life now. 'Look at me, Annabelle, you will walk free from here, but your silence must remain, for the rest of your days.'

Her eyes shivered. She heard me, whether she understood, was a different matter.

'I saw them.'

'You what?' I could hardly hear her whisper through the groaning gaol.

'I saw them, so I'm here, they were leaving that place.' Her deep voice worried me. There was more to this girl than at first met my eye.

'What place?'

Her eyes looked at me; the moment she said those words, I felt a cold shiver run through my very soul.

'They took a boy, the boy who was taken by the hangman, they took him to the place, the place with the stone lion.'

I took a step back, feeling the bitterness hit me. 'Where is this place?'

Her eyes filled with saddened tears; I could see she was struggling to simply breathe. 'I can't remember. They were the same men who wanted the orchard, that's why I'm going to die, because they want the land I wouldn't sell.'

The walk home took me through many streets, Annabelle had said enough, I would push her no further, I would save the questions until she was safely away from the gaol.

I walked far through the town that night, I recall seeing Mrs Bennet, a high-class woman of particularly good reputation, she bid me a good evening, she knew many in the town, it was her duty to know the executioner, as vulgar a business as it was.

Friar Lane was oddly calm that evening. The sun set over the distant lands, a feeling of peace, serenity, was in the breeze. The late evening saw me through to Carter Gate, a part of the town I cannot recall venturing before, travelling towards Hockley, my eyes watered, a large building at the front of me showed the symbol I had searched so long for, the place that Billy was frightened of; the place that had sent Annabelle to her death.

The building was stunningly ordinary. Meeting on the corner of Goose Gate and Broad Lane, two stone lions glared towards the town in front. Upon approaching the building, the stone lions above the door brought fear into my heart, a sinking knowledge that I had found the place of suffering.

The blue door opened, startling me. I stepped back, and that was when my heart truly sank.

'Evening, George,' said Godfrey, fully dressed and ready for an evening with the watch. He stepped from the building, a large smile widened his smug face.

'Godfrey,' I nodded.

'What brings you down here?'

It stumped me, I thought hard, desperately searching for an excuse to be that far away from home. He knew my routine.

'The father-in-law, he's insisted on finding a new property, enough for us all to reside, a small house like the one I have is no longer ample enough, I am on the search for new property, and I know the houses here are much larger.'

I could see Godfrey thinking his suspicion was clear, but even he dare not question the town executioner, especially outside a building which was gaining a poor reputation.

'Perhaps try Coal Pitt Lane, I hear the land has been divided, to build your own may work out better for you.'

'That's a fine idea.' I gave a brimming smile, removing his suspicion. They began their walk into the town, and so I walked with them, to ensure the suspicion was removed further.

'I was thinking of Chesterfield Lane, it's quiet, but has a decent link towards the town.'

'For now perhaps, but the new mills will be here soon. It won't be long until that entire half of town is taken by mills and works.' He had a valid point; one I couldn't argue. I was not even looking for property, but our chatting of different areas of the town, had me thinking.

With only a few months before I would pay my debt, my wages would double. Working as a gaoler paid the bills enough, working as an executioner was a bonus on top of that, a single hanging would see us fit for more than a month.

Arriving back at my small home, I bid farewell to the watchmen, who had provided a decent insight into property in the town.

'We're moving!' I announced.

Roderick firmly sat at the table clutching his cup, Isabelle was in her usual place by the fire in the kitchen. A smell of broth warmed me to my core.

'What do you mean, moving?' she asked, placing the few plates on the table.

'Well, having dad staying here is wonderful.' I was truly blessed to have my family by my side, especially my extended family. 'But, he has been sharing a room with the children, it is hardly fair, Issy, a debt will be paid soon, we can afford better property, I see there are new works along Gregory's paddock, we could look there, or even the new buildings in Sneinton.'

Isabelle looked at her father, who raised his brows in agreement. Sleeping on a cold wooden floor with nowt but thin padding beneath him was not good for a man his age.

'I am living as a pauper,' he said with a wide grin. He looked towards me, an immediate apology was in his eyes. 'I mean nothing by that.'

'My parents had a pauper's burial, Dad, but it was to benefit me and Issy. I have no shame in their sacrifice. As you well know yourself, the rich and poor lie equal in the garden of God.'

'Indeed, they do, but I am not ready for the garden of God yet. A little comfort is welcome for old bones.'

'There we are. Your father agrees, so, unfortunately, you have no say, Issy,' I mocked.

Giving a hard thump in my side, she looked at her father. 'Very well, I suppose I live with old men. A home must also provide for them.'

The weekend would still see me within the gaol. I had agreed to work a Saturday, to cover for loss of gaolers.

An outbreak of fever in the town had them worried. I did not worry about such things.

Cleanliness was God's cure to ailments such as this. I was sure to keep myself washed to perfection, if only I could say the same for my children.

I visited with Annabelle that morning, I tried to whisper our plan to her, but her broken self, remained silent, I begged her to stay quiet about our plan, and I promised her, I would do all I could about the building with the stone lion, she did not respond to me.

The bells of the town accompanied my walk back home. I needed Annabelle to speak, to listen. She had remained mute. Women were always difficult creatures for me to understand, I was a quiet boy growing up, when I met Isabelle, she did all the talking for me. I always knew when to step in on conversation, but Isabelle was always the one to guide me.

'I need your help.'

Isabelle sat at the table, trying to sew together the last few bits of rope for the women's jacket.

'What this time?' she moaned; I could see the sore marks on her fingers as she forced the needle through the last bit of rope.

'Annabelle.'

'The condemned?'

'Yes, she won't speak to me, at all. She sees I'm there. She must, but I cannot get a response from her.'

She softened her eyes, looking over her shoulder. 'And you're surprised by this?' She stopped sewing and turned. Surprised by my stupidity. 'She was raped by a man, arrested by men, and sentenced to hang by a man. Now any man who comes forwards, even offering a saviour, she has no reason to ever trust a man again.'

I sat at the table; I could hear Roderick calling to the children outside. 'Then what am I to do?'

Isabelle took a moment to think. 'I suppose the only thing you can do, is get her to trust you, get her to understand, to speak to her properly, remember, she is not weak, she has shown more strength than the man who sentenced her, more strength than the man who defiled her, and more strength than any gaoler in that place.'

She was right, and I daren't argue. She was a powerful woman. Isabelle had the frame of a weak woman, but I knew her mind. It was frightening, powerful. Women were often seen as absent minded little folk, but I knew them as something different.

We were alone the night that Geoffrey was born, I knew I needed to help Isabelle, and what I saw, forced my belief in women for good, her suffering, the pain she endured with courage and might, there not a creature alive as strong as a woman.

The church offered us a pleasant morning, Father Donahue had decided on a lighter sermon, allowing us to enjoy the delights of some modern music, of course we had heard most of it before, but a new wave of music had made its way into the church, I did not understand a single word the man was singing, but it was pleasingly different.

The sun beamed that morning, offering a new light, readying us for a new week. No children had been scheduled, which was lucky for us. Removing a woman from the gaol would prove more difficult, especially one which seemed unable to listen or learn.

'I remember you, selling bushels on the Weekday Cross. I also remember your mother being with you a few times. How is she now?' Her silence broke to a small nod. 'I know this is hard for you, Annabelle, but I'm trying to help you. I am trying to get you free of this place, but for you to do that, I need you to listen.' Her red eyes looked towards me. 'Annabelle, you have the strength of a woman, which is more than any man I know, please, I need you to find the strength now to listen, my wife works tirelessly, so we can save you, and have you free from this place.'

'How?' She had refused food for days; her hunger was turning her towards insanity.

'The only way for you to be free from this place, is for you to die.' Her eyes fled towards the cold floor on which she sat. 'But you won't die. You just have to make it look like you do. When you're boxed, upon the morrow you will be free from this place, able to walk free from Nottingham for good.'

'And my parents?' her voice quivered. 'I am unwed. I sacrificed my life with a husband to see my aging parents to a comfortable end. I gave my life to them—'

'And now, you get your life back, if you wish I can arrange that you mother meets you when you are free of the gaol, or, you may be free of her also, I shall give you the day to think, later, please eat, it will help convince them of your death.'

Her eyes lit as I left. I could see her life returning to her pale skin, her reddening eyes flourished. God would save her.

The Monday morning was a strange day, we would spare Annabelle until the Wednesday. Only God knows why Francis chose a midweek hanging of a woman.

A heavy summer rain pelted the pavement outside, Isabelle spent the night attempting to rescue the floor from the leaking roof, 'twould be awhile yet, until we could look for a better accommodation, until then, the house would be covered with pots and pans, catching raindrops.

The children thought it highly amusing, seeing me running from the house with my coat pulled over my head. Upon reaching the gaol I was as drowned as a Leen rat. Even the gaolers looked on in amusement.

'Keep laughing,' I chalked, 'you're walking back in this shortly.' Their laughter soon died, realising the weather would get to them as well.

Setting my uniform to dry over the laundry racking, I placed a gown on. It wouldn't take too long for my garments to dry, given the large fire which heated the laundry. Settling down to some tea, I began reading a paper left by a gaoler.

'*The proper persons are now appointed to protect the same, and all offenders taking Fish out of the said river, by Nets or otherwise, will henceforth be prosecuted.*

Any persons giving notice of such offender or offenders will, upon their conviction, be handsomely rewarded, upon application made to Mr. John Sleight,

Park-Keeper, at Wollaton, Wollaton house, 20th April 1811.'

Someone had also lost their dog Nell, which was more interesting news than the desperate poachers to me.

The rain continued battering the yard outside. With my garments finally dried, I proceeded upon my rounds, where I came across quite some pleasant chatting that day. The unexpected shower lightened some spirits that noon.

The end cell brought a chill to me, but even then, as I peered into the cell, my heart skipped, upon seeing Annabelle feasting upon a bowl of gruel, although it was not the most pleasing of meals, it would strengthen her for a hanging.

'So, you took my advice.'

'I don't want to go back.' Were her words to me, a soft, sorrowful glint of the eye caused me great sorrow.

'To your parents?'

She nodded her weakened head. 'This would've been a relief for me.' Her croaking voice brought no echo through the halls, a pleasing situation for a man of the law who was discussing breaking it. 'My father always insisted I remained homebound, tied to a chair practically. My mother, always too drunk or weak to stand up to him, mother's ruin is still prevalent in our home.'

'So, the daughter of a drunk and abuser, you certainly deserve a second chance of life.'

'But where will I go?' She begged. She knew only the art of selling apples. They were poor as well. Better quality was found along Mansfield Road. I did not wish to dampen her further.

'Leave that part to me.'

'I am not a wealthy woman, I cannot even leave the hangman a tip, I cannot even afford to die.'

'Worry not.' I leant towards her. She did not know who I was. 'The hangman requires nothing from you of monetary value, Annabelle. I am the hangman, and I am your way out.'

'Why are you doing this?' her soft whispering voice quivered.

'Because God does not want you yet, you have been wronged, and I am a man who can put it right. All you need to do, is listen, and follow everything I say. Can you do that?'

She gave a quick nod; her silence spoke of the desperate fate which had been placed by her feet. I looked at the side of me, ensuring no one could hear, not even the prisoners who remained laughing and singing in their cells.

I showed Annabelle all I could. She, too, found it highly amusing to see the town executioner acting a fate he hoped he would never see. I even took a noose at one point, to show her properly of the redness required, the proper way to die, but in doing so, I assured her, her life would be spared, by God, and the family God had chosen for his work.

The rain battered the steps that day. God was testing me, Roderick was worried. He saw the crowds gathering close to the steps of the gallery. She would need to act well; her audience was waiting.

Stone ice rain pattered the steps along High Pavement. A disturbance on Narrow Marsh had many of the gaolers busy, but the crowd still gathered.

It was a strange one. They knew the girl well. The crowd formed a bond with her. Her tears streamed as they led her onto the steps. Her eyes looked at me.

She mouthed the words, 'I'm scared.'

I mouthed the words back, 'Good.'

I had to be brutal with this one. She was not showing the same emotion as the children would, they barely understood the gift they had been given. Annabelle knew exactly what her gift was, she struggled to remain without laughter, placing the noose over her head. I heard a boasting boo from the crowd. An elderly man wandered towards the back of the crowd; his crooked bones carried him towards the Weekday Cross. I paid no heed.

Roderick took his place beside where her body would flail. She dropped, a perfect struggle and a sigh of relief from myself and Roderick. The flailing stopped; the crowd dispersed. Placing her onto splinted linen, we carried her back inside.

The cold room beside the yard was empty, cold. Her rustling broke the silence of the room on the table.

'What now?' she whispered.

Roderick and I stood either side of the table. She remained lying down. 'Now the hard part, y dear,' said Roderick.

'You must remain silent, in the box, we will put you in, nail the coffin lid shut, on the morrow, Roderick here will take you to the Marshes, before you reach the marsh, my wife, Isabelle, she will await you in an alleyway, from there you will be taken to sanctuary.' I leant close towards her, stroking her rain drenched face. 'Worry not, a few more hours, and you will be with a man of God. He will see your freedom from there.'

'Thank you, a thousand times, I thank you.'

'You can never return here. If anyone sees you, that will put many at risk. We all risk our lives to save you, you are not alone in this world, Annabelle. God's family is with you.'

She was somewhat stricken with my words, as if a bolt of lightning had stricken her. Her silence was welcome that evening, her escape was again to perfection. The family God had chosen, had again proven its worth.

Chapter Five Gallows Hill

Francis walked much lighter that morning. There had been no hangings for over a month, I could feel something in the air. He was brimming, needing to see the suffering by his unfair hand.

His chambers beamed with an unfair sunlight; such a place should have been as grim as its occupant.

'It is a fine morning, George.'

I stood by his window, wondering why he had called me there. 'God's light certainly shines bright this day.'

He sniggered as he turned. 'Please, God remains free of a town as tainted as this one.' He walked to his desk, readying his papers for the day. 'The works along Mansfield Road are almost complete, allowing us to reopen Gallows Hill.'

The name sent a shiver through me, knowing our plan would have to change.

'Gallows Hill?' I tried to throw him off, giving a chuckle within my reply. 'May I speak freely, Francis?'

He widened his eyes, appreciating my good manners. 'Gallows Hill is a place of somewhat ill repute, we set it aside as barbaric long ago, if this town is to be seen as civilised, a place of high society, such displays of barbarism should remain away from the prying eyes of the public. I agree there are certain lessons which should always be shown, so a murderer should be executed along the steps of the fine Kings court, however, executing a child, in view of a thirsty crowd, it shows this place will never be more than a downtrodden town.'

'Your father's honesty has caught with you, George. I shall think of your words and opinion. It is appreciated that the town executioner thinks of such things as high society.'

'We are simply trying to create a better future for our fine town, and by God's grace, it may one day see us as a city of morals.'

'You bother me, George.' His words concerned me, furrowing my brow as I froze to listen. 'Here I believed you were a simple family man, the work you do is in no doubt practiced, yet I believed you were here for the wage, all along you were here to build alongside me, come, let us see what filth the gutter has for us.'

Frank highly frowned upon theft. He hated poor men. The first to see the stand was a man called Collin Gilmoor, a pockmarked face under a head of grease filled hair. He had seen better days, which probably ended in his youth.

Charged to a flogging along the town lines, this would be a duty I would enjoy, given he was caught attempting to take cattle from a nearby farm. I know the farmer there, lovely man. He would've given Collin all the sustenance he needed, even employment if he had asked.

Lessons were something all had to learn, 'twas why God graced us upon this earth. I had learnt my lesson through gambling.

The town silence unnerved me that evening. My debt was near paid, I could continue my search for property. Roderick had joined my side that evening to aide me in my search.

Roderick led the way, taking us towards several large houses. A house on Hockley gave me a shuddering feeling.

'A moment.' I stopped, hoping Roderick would help me place the pieces together. 'A while ago, a boy within the gaol, he told me of a building with a stone lion. Annabelle told me the same, the building holds some unfavoured reputation.'

Roderick looked at the unsuspecting building. 'This one?' He pointed towards it. A small symbol above the door below the stone lion made him chuckle. 'Oh,

George, you are too good a man to be seen in such a place.'

'What is it?'

'This, my son, is a place of Gentlemen, 'tis a gentlemen's chambers, a place where those of high society go to get away with whatever atrocities their coins will afford them.'

'So why would I see lawmen coming from this place?'

'Because if you wish to remain above the law, you must see every slight piece of illness this town offers, if you know their secrets, you know their sins, and no man will punish a man with fewer sins than he.'

His knowledge fascinated me. I knew such places existed, 'twas how I became so ill-fated in the first place. I had learnt my lesson, and now, I wished to see the lawmen learn theirs.

'Do you believe I could ever be welcomed within a place such as this?'

'Of course, everyone with sin wishes to be acquainted with the executioner. It would be a pity to see your talent wasted. George, fit well with the judge, and he will see you well within these walls.'

'A property first, perhaps. We need to appear as men of good fortune before placing ourselves into the lion's den. Tell me, do you see any you like?'

He shook his head; a downward smile gave off a feeling of disappointed anguish.

'I have checked the papers. All that seems worthy are farms. Property within the town is scarce. Perhaps your thought of building was correct.'

'Twas not my thought, but the thought of Godfrey, a lawman who frequents this very place.'

We continued our way from the town, heading towards the farms along Broad Lane. Many farmers were wishing to sell their lands, given that so much industry had seen their farms to waste, they believed a sale would save their businesses, but the town was going a different way, it was heading towards a city status.

'Did you find anything?' Isabelle asked with excitement.

'Father!' Geoffrey screamed as he came running. Panic swelled him. Fear took my breath. 'A boy outside, he's being led to the gaol, he did nothing wrong, you have to help him!'

'What happened?' I hurriedly asked, following Geoffrey to the yard outside.

A small alleyway took me towards St Peters Gate. 'He was looking, he got close to Mrs Bakers breads, but he took nothing!'

'Calm yourself, Geoff.' I turned and crouched before him. 'Another of God's children, if his punishment leads him to my rope, we will be there to see him free.'

Geoffrey instantly calmed. Looking at his trousers, I could see he'd had another day playing near the local farms. 'Go clean yourself, and take your sister. We must always look presentable. If we are to continue God's work, things are to change.'

I did not believe my words to be harsh, but something disappointed the boy. He hardly spoke to me over dinner that evening.

'The children are to take lessons in the town. I know of several tutors, close to the church, schooling is not something I believe is befitting of such talented minds.' I looked at the children, they remained silent. 'I shall be visiting the hall on the morrow, to make application for land, a new home to be built upon it, befitting a family of God—' Their silence bothered me, — 'What is the matter with you two?'

'I would rather see school, father, there are other children there,' begged Geoffrey.

'Yes, children of this town whose father I have seen upon the stand, whose mother has faced the accusations of a drunkard, I cannot see my children in the hands of such people, Mrs Kemp, she is a wonderful teacher—'

'She is only interested in works of God.' Geoffrey's bitterness hurt me.

'What is the issue with that?'

'There is no issue, father. Lessons of the lord are something I always wish to hear of, but what of lessons of arithmetic, lessons of geography?'

'Of reading and writing, I see your concern. I shall have you placed in the care of Mr Ross, 'twas his father taught me as a bane. I trust his perseverance has been passed down.'

'Ah, I see.' Isabelle leant toward Geoffrey. 'Your father was not the easiest of students. I vaguely remember an argument, tween him and his teacher, telling his teacher he made an error with his spellings. Of course the teacher was right.'

'Alright, I think the boy gets it. I was never easy growing up, 'twas why I became so quiet.' I too leant towards Geoffrey. 'I discovered at a young age, to avoid the cane, know their idiocy in your mind only, speaking will often leave you with a sore rear.'

Geoffrey eased that evening, his frown melted to a smile. He loved his family, but the child baffled me. Whilst Geoffrey would always care for his family, he had a care for all. He had his mother's need to save them all. Bethany was a quiet child, just like her father.

The next morning saw the unfortunate boy toward the stand. Francis was in a light mood that morning.

'Theft?' Francis spat as he looked toward the prosecution. 'Of what, exactly? Air?'

'My lord, we saw the boy skulking. We caught him in the act, Sir.'

'Poppycock.' Francis leant back. I thought it rather odd, until I saw it. The boy was well dressed, a rich red overcoat, clean black shorts, and shined shoes. He held status.

'Marcus, you are free to go from here boy, I deeply apologise for the upset this has caused.' He saw the prosecution step forwards from the corner of his eye, his head twisted, the prosecution froze like a caught rabbit.

'I know this boy, theft is not in his blood, I shall be having harsh words with the sheriff's men.'

It placed Francis in an ill mood for the rest of the day. However, no blood would be spilt that day, or any others to follow.

Sat alone with Isabelle at the table, I gazed at her.

'How are plans going?' I asked.

'The builders are proving troublesome,' she sighed her reply. 'I was born with the wrong appendage for them to take instruction from me, they insist on first speaking to my husband.'

'Ludicrous,' I huffed, I supported Isabelle in all she did, including her silent fight over equality. 'I will speak with them on the morrow, if they cause more issues I will make it clear that their contract will terminate.'

'Thank you,' she said with a soft smile. 'It isn't difficult work. Not like that which faces you and father.'

I reached out, placing my hand on her. 'We can handle it, your father is brilliant at this, even I were shocked he has taken to it so easily.'

'You didn't expect him to?'

I shook my head. 'I don't know what I expected, really. Some fail at their first hanging, others discover something about themselves they'd rather never have known.'

'And you?'

'Me, I keep it so closely guarded, any feelings are so tightly packed inside I don't know what I feel anymore, or even if I do,' I chuckled.

She reached over, holding my hand tighter.

'You're a good man, George, and a wonderful husband and father, but it isn't healthy to keep it all inside, you can talk to me.'

I tightly smiled at her, those dazzling eyes of innocence I could never burden with my misery.

'This is all I need, Issy, you, your father and the children, you drown it all, the moment I step through that door.'

The cool cobbles clacking beneath my shoes welcomed me towards Hockley that evening, my plans were in place. Isabelle found the builders, the land, and begat employing plans for new accommodation in an affluent area of Sneinton, this would give us ample land, enough for a small holding, if Isabelle wished for such.

Slowly, I was becoming a gentleman, the type of man Francis would long to see in his company.

The lions glared towards me that evening, the terror on their faces caught me, thinking of those who had seen it before me, 'twas the symbol of Billy's suffering, it made me wonder, how many others had seen such horror in the faces of the lions.

A window at the side showed a small face glaring out, a small woman, a strange thing to see in a place built for gentlemen.

Roderick had failed to join me at the gaol that day. He was feeling tired after a week of planning the structure of the new home.

The large handle in the centre of the blue door turned. As the heavy door creaked open, a familiar face caught me off guard.

'George!' Francis called out to me. I would've headed away from him. The hour was pressing towards ten. 'What has you this way?'

'I was visiting with my architect.' I was becoming well with lying. 'I noticed the stone lion. Above the door, it's a craftsmanship I hope to find within my property.'

'Certainly.' He turned and admired the grotesque face of the lions. 'I can put you in good standing with the mason, if you wish of course.'

'You would do that?' I brimmed with glee, 'twas all an act. 'That would be most kind, Francis.'

'Not at all.' His boasting unnerved me as he ruffled the neck of his cloak.

'Are you returning home?'

He nodded, a croak caught his voice, 'I can only take so much pleasure of an evening.'

'Of course, come. I must see you home. The town is safe when the law is a foot. I am yet to see them though. I would not forgive myself if something befell you.'

'I do not take your offer as offensive, George, you're rather much larger than I. An old man like me could often use an acquaintance.'

I would've left him with his carriage along Cow Lane. Instead, he invited me in, offering a conversation along the way. I believed his house was not far.

The path towards the judge's house was paved with gold. Along the side of the road, large gatherings of flowers laid. A magistrate received a handsome salary. His home was a marvel of sorts, stretching far along a dirt path, a gargantuan beast upon the skyline. He was very well off, so well off, in fact, it would take me near on an hour to return to my home.

His carriage took me to the outskirts, leaving me at the top of Mansfield Road. The judge lived alone, with over fifteen bedrooms. It made me wonder who else lived in the company of such a miserable old man.

The return home was gruelling. Every road offered nothing but darkness. Highwaymen frequented the area. Gallows Hill soon came into sight, taking me back towards town.

'The boy is fine,' I burst as I came through the door. The children had been sent to bed long ago. I knew Isabelle would still be awake, given she would never sleep without me.

'That's a relief,' she said with a sigh. She turned to see my grim looking face. 'What ever is the matter, Love?'

Roderick turned; his brows raised.

'The boy is fine, because his father is a member of high society; his father is one of the chambers supporters, a close friend of the family also, Frank was furious to see him upon the stand.'

'A firm tongue lashing in the lion's den, I can only assume,' said Roderick, turning back to the bowl of stew Isabelle placed down.

'Surely, that would not have you saddened?'

'No, a boy was saved, which is a reason to be glad, and yet, if it were a pauper's boy, accused of the same crime, with the same evidence, he would be upon my rope within a week.' I lumped to the chair by the side of Roderick. 'The unfairness shows far too prevalent.'

'The only change we can make is to save single lives, we will not change society.' I could tell Isabelle felt bad for my situation. 'I know you wish to change the world, but change too much, and there will be no world left for us, George.'

'I do not wish for a world of inequality.'

'Neither do I, but we do what we can,' she replied as she sat. 'I'm frightened,' she burst, looking at me and her father. 'There are new plans to build along Pepper Street, it gets busier each day, and I fear I may be caught.'

I placed my spoon down, not wanting to continue until her mind was free from fear.

'We will find another way, there are lanes all the way towards the marshes, we can use any of them.'

'Work in the town is increasing. Each day a new stone structure engulfs the town, the boarders are widening. Soon the river will become a hindrance.'

Her panic struck me.

'And that is why we are needed, to bring fairness.'

'Do you ever wonder why?' asked Roderick who had been relatively quiet.

'Why what?' I asked.

He sighed. 'There was a time, when London, full of disease and suffering, it needed vital changes, but no one would allow those changes. Small homes were in the way of industry and change, so, it is believed that the government set a great fire, ridding the streets of plague, but taking most of the buildings as well, giving them chance to rebuild.'

'What you're saying is, something much darker is at play.'

'Of course it is,' said Isabelle, 'something darker is always at play.'

'The men of this town, the men of the gentlemen's club, they are investors. Land is worth its weight in gold at the moment.'

'But when a poor man stands in your way, or an orchard, you do whatever you can to get it, if greed takes you down that path.' My understanding was clear.

'Greed overpowers necessity,' said Isabelle. 'Which is another problem I bring to you gentlemen. The father at the church is asking for help, there is only so much he can do, paying for their transport to other places has depleted his funds. We must find a way of making extra.'

The industry of lace was a rich industry. The highly sort after material had gained increased popularity with the masses, the highest of the high were clad in Nottingham Lace, even to the extent of our regent George.

I would've been proud of my town, were it not so tainted by poorly broken men, who wished for nothing but to line their pockets with each other's coin.

My way home that evening again took me through the back streets of Hockley. I was hoping to see Francis exiting the lion's den; I was lucky that evening. I did have a plan in mind, but my plan would unknowingly take me through the darkest of times.

'Evening, George.' He stepped from the building; I gave a wide, pompous smile bouncing towards him. 'Seems to be a habit of late.'

'It sure is,' I chuckled, 'another meeting with my architect. Sadly, I believe this shall be our last meeting. The details are to be left with Isabelle.'

'Your wife?' he sounded surprised. 'And here was me believing you to be a man of intellect,' he mocked. His mocking rattled my bones, feeling my blood heat in the moment.

'Isabelle excels in the art of detail.'

'As do most women; but matters of such importance should never be left to a woman.' We began a slow walk towards his carriage, which awaited him along Cow Lane.

'You may think her just a woman, but I have seen her at her worst and her best—'

'Lucky you, before Charlotte passed, I hardly saw her at all.' It was a strange revelation; I did not even know he was once married. 'Her days were filled with entertaining others, never time for a husband.'

I could not blame the woman he spoke so coldly of; a husband such as he would offer nothing but a reason to flee.

'You are a man of great stature; she would need to keep people close to see you grow in society.'

'Well, the mayor was always a favourite of hers, no matter which one it was.' His mocking of a dead woman churned at my gut, but I needed to remain in the character I had created.

'Isabelle has my best interests at heart, and the interests of her family, 'tis why she insisted upon a private education for the children, I saw a property along Coal Pitt Lane, but she insisted upon the new buildings in Sneinton for our new home, says it is a place of built repute.'

'Built repute,' he sniggered, 'your wife amuses me. The executioner will dine alongside magistrates, lords and ladies, of the highest order. It sounds to me you have made a fine choice in women.'

We arrived at the carriage, I jumped to open the door for him. The snivelling judge was my only way into the lion's den. My eyes begged, but I remained humble in my need.

'Thank you, George,' he groaned, struggling into the carriage. He settled upon the seat, smoothing his cloak down. His grim light eyes looked towards me.

'Tell you what, if you are through with your work, why not join me tomorrow evening? At the chambers, at least then it will save you from meeting me at the door with an attempt to enter.'

I had been found out; I felt a grin as I looked at the cobbles. 'It would mark a memorable occasion, but only if you're sure.'

'A man like you, George, you belong in the chambers of the Lions, bring with you the sum of twenty pounds, it shall see your lifetime entry to the chambers.' He leant towards me. 'With a man of such standing, you will see it as a worthy investment. Feel free to bring Roderick, we are always on the search for worthy patrons of the chambers.'

I was elated as his carriage rolled down the cobbles of Cow Lane. I could finally view the atrocities for myself.

Rushing home, the children were again in bed. Isabelle sat at the table, her arms folded in front of her, her delicate head rested upon them.

I took a seat beside her; Roderick had also retired early that evening. I whispered her name, hoping to rouse her.

Her flickering eyes opened; a beaming smile met me. I would've told her then, she was exhausted. To plague her with such knowledge would only tire her further.

She quickly stood, ready to make something warm for me for supper.

'It's alright, I've already eaten. Come, sleep calls us both.'

She was reluctant to turn. She held her head low.

'George, I have news.' She slowly turned to face me, clutching a cloth as she did. Her smile again beamed. 'I visited with Mrs Morledge today. I have been feeling unwell of late, a tightening in the belly.' My heart raced; I could feel my eyes burning with unwilling tears. 'She could confirm my suspicion.' Her smile became laughter. 'I expect a few months, and our family will again grow.'

Elated, I ran to her, wanting to lift her I feared for the damage I could do. She was so small compared to me.

Her concern was clear. She looked at me with dewdrop eyes.

'What this means for our cause, I am yet to work out, but we will do all we can, we will continue to save God's children.'

'Our family is blessed, not only with another child, but with a wife and mother, as wonderful as you, Oh, Issy, what I did to deserve such grace I will never know, I am so proud to call you my wife.'

'And I am proud to call you my husband.' She wrapped her small arms around me. I never thought I would see such strength from a creature so small.

'I also have news.' Her excitement had me unhinged; I did not think of my words before I said them. 'The judge has invited me into the Lions Chambers. I am to take twenty pounds with me tomorrow. He has also welcomed your father.'

'Then you must be doing something right. That place is reserved for the most iniquitous of men, of which you certainly are not one. I know my husband.'

'I'm glad you do. I shall make every attempt to keep my appearances there to a minimum, especially if you need help in the home.'

'I have the children for that. Besides, with a new property, we will have plenty of kind neighbours wanting to know the executioner's wife.' Her mocking of my duty amused me, simply because 'twas true. Those of high society had more sins than most, they would need a friend in the gaol when those sins surfaced. Who better than the judge, jury and executioner.

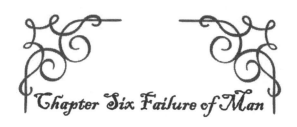

Chapter Six Failure of Man

*I*t was a gross miscalculation on my part. Believing that the chambers were filled with sordid men, I instead stepped into the large bar filled with darkened smoke. A few red tables surrounded with good men of the town.

The smell of ale was absent here, they chose the finer things, amber spirits were served from a round bar in the centre of the room, a large staircase led to some upper rooms, I paid little attention to them as I made my way towards the bar.

'What are you doing, George?' sniggered Francis.

'I was hoping for some drinks before we settle.'

'This is a gentleman's chambers, George. The drinks will be brought to you. 'tis not a commonplace. We are treated with proper respect here.'

Proper respect was something I was yet to see from the servers, a constant look of terror upon their faces was clear to me, the others failed to see it, I knew what fear looked like, it came in many forms, but it was still fear.

There were plenty of men there. All looked at me with fearful pride.

'Oh, so you finally caught him,' said a tall redheaded man. His jacket matched his crimson hair and cheeks.

'Didn't take long, David.' Francis looked towards me, holding a deck of silver cards. They lay a few dice on the table. 'I believe the chambers are now complete, George. This is David. He was once a highly skilled Luddite. He now lends his craft to the hiring in the mills.'

'A Luddite?' It shocked me to see someone of such lower class there, a man who had gained an excellent reputation in the business of textiles, surely was not good enough to be rubbing elbows with magistrates and watchmen.

'I was once, as Frank said, I now lend my talent to the hiring of skilled workers. I do not take offence at the name, either. To be known as a Luddite means I give heart to those who are stepped on by design.'

'Skilled workers are hard to find in such an industry. Besides, with the uprising in the industry, I find it rather odd to see a man of such reputation not quivering elsewhere.'

'You amuse me, George,' he chuckled, taking a step back. 'I am a Luddite at heart, and we are here to stay, the machines of industry are unreliable, the hands of men and women are far more superior, if you were a betting man, you would see a bet upon the Luddites.'

'Well, I was a betting man, which saw me to ruin, I appear to be poor at it, so, were I to place a bet upon the Luddites, they would see me hanged for bringing their misfortune, I can only wish you the best in your future endeavours.'

We watched David walk towards some men gathered at a table on the other side of the bar. I could feel the stone-cold glare from Francis at the side of me.

'My honesty shocks you?'

'It concerns me, George.' Francis's hushed tone told me I had stepped out of place. 'He may be just a Luddite, but his father still has property along the borders of Sherwood. He will be a lord when his father passes.'

I leant to see David speaking with some other well-dressed men.

'Regardless, the Luddites are ended, the machines he speaks of, they may not produce quality, but they produce quantity, and cheap too, the people of this town are not all property owners, they have expenses, men like him fail to see it, and that is why the machines will win. To call himself a Luddite with heart alone, it is like calling yourself an angel of god, because you once gave bread to a poor man.'

'I cannot argue with you. I have seen their downfall since the argument sprang, but David will be an issue for us. He knows law, and he knows fairness. He is attempting to pass a fair wages bill through parliament.'

'It will be to no avail, parliament have much more trying matters than dealing with a man who knits ladies stockings for a living.'

My mockery was winning Francis over. It was a pleasant evening; the Chambers offered a better company than the roads outside.

The stage on the left of the chambers gave a red and golden glow, as a glorious young woman stepped on to it. Her voice was like that of a quivering angel, she held fear deep within her voice, a darkness in her eyes sent a shiver through me, she had seen something I never wanted to know. Something in her face sent a piercing shadow into me, but the room lit with the sound of her voice.

'You like her?' asked Francis as he leant forwards.

'Very much so,' I replied, as innocently as any man could.

'I will have a word, see if you can gain some company with her one evening,' he said as he sat back.

The young girl made her way back up the well-polished staircase and into her room, giving one last glance to the patrons below who cheered drunkenly.

'I apologise, I don't get what you mean?'

'You can request an audience with her, an hour to do as you wish,' he replied with his brows raised.

I slammed my body back and straightened. 'No,' I stammered, 'That an awful thought, Francis, I would never, she is a child! And I'm married.'

He took a cigar from the side of his pocket, immediately a steward lit it.

'Nobel of you, but through her performance your eyes were hooked, George.'

'To the beauty of her voice, nothing more, I did not believe you thought so ill of me?'

'I do not,' said Francis with a huff as he sat forwards. 'Rose is a stunning creature. Her voice is but a bonus.' A light sweat clutched his brow.

'I would never think of doing any such thing, Francis, please, look at me better in the future.'

'I apologise if I have offended you,' he said with a bow of his head. 'She is wonderful, and the rules are clear, she is a companion only, we see no ladies of the evening here.'

'Even so, to be in a room a lone with a young woman is forbidden, or at least it should be.'

Francis chuckled, 'You sound like my father.'

'Then your father was a very sane man.'

'Calm down, George, she is only a woman,' he sniggered.

I could say nothing more, such callous behaviour towards a young girl provided clarity on the type of establishment we were in.

Upon preparing to leave, a small, slim man came through the door, a long grey overcoat covered to his neck. Raindrops upon his coat warned of harsh weather outside. The man walked through the chambers, heading straight up the stairs.

'What's up there?'

Francis's eyes followed the man. 'This is a gentleman's chamber, George, up there is whatever you wish.'

His bitter words were still with me. Billy had promised to be a good boy, to not scream or cause upset or alarm.

My evenings at the chambers were drawing me closer to the truth. They cared not for who they spoke to, or how loud they spoke. The men in that place didn't bother hiding their sins, only the rooms along the balcony hid the actual sins of the Lion's Chambers.

Isabelle awaited my arrival that evening. Her belly had grown over the days. I had been withdrawn from her of late. I left the chambers for a few days, to catch up on some needed family time.

I told her, 'The morrow brings us church, a place of contemplation, and I have much to contemplate.' We sat together on the large sofa; her head laid upon my lap in the fire's comfort.

'And what contemplation is this?'

'I know what that place is now, the Lion's Chambers as they call it, they have rooms there, where men go to feed their sins, but some of those rooms, I know they hold more than women, they hold others like Billy.' I stroked my fingers through her delicate hair, the small curls ruffled through my fingers.

'Well, then what would you suggest?'

I did not know what she was asking, but I knew God had a plan.

'He will not let them suffer for long. God has a plan for all.'

'If God's plan is something you rely on, perhaps it won't be such a terrible idea to have our own?' She sat straight, holding her belly. 'George, I understand that what we do is limited, but what if it wasn't? We live in the county of beggars and thieves, but also of heroes and good men.'

'You seem rather adamant.'

'Because I am.'

I could see her thinking, a pain in her voice she tried to hide, but she could hide nothing from me.

'Before we began this, before the boy Billy you told me of, you were half the man you are today.' Her glistening eyes shone in the flickering hue of the candles. 'George, I love you, and it is a true love that will be broken by none, I gave my life to God, and my loyalty to you, all I want is to see you peaceful, and that place, it will not please you, knowing what happens there, I only pray, you will find peace in the arms of your family, we are always here for you, George, you do not walk this world alone.'

Her concern was clear, she was attempting to ward me away from the aristocracy. Roderick was a different kind of man. He was a landowner, a man of engineering. When I met Isabelle, I was working for Roderick, helping keep the poachers away from the cattle on his farms. It was my duty as a watchman to keep the farm safe, I soon spread into the village.

I remember the night I saw her. I was neither the age of eleven, charged with the duty to patrol the farm into the late evening, I believed her to be a poacher when I first saw her creeping shadow, I hid within a hedgerow, pouncing upon her shadow as she crept close to the farm.

Her first words to me were, 'well done, your duty is done, you caught the farmer's daughter.' The blush on my face burnt as I stood. Begging she not tell her father of my misdeed, she insisted on telling him, believing it would impress him, and she was right.

Isabelle had a way of being right. She was a bricky girl when I met her, she remained as such. Roderick took an instant liking to me, knowing I would tackle any who threatened his farm. I still do not know what possessed her to be out at an hour so late, skulking around the farm.

Rain, it was a usual sight for this time of year. As the autumn crept towards us, fear was in the hearts of many. The autumn harvest approached. It had been a dry summer, very little rain was now in contrast to the constant flurry of cold rain.

Rushing to the church, we quickly warmed on the cold pews. Father Donahue frowned towards his congregation. His sermons were usually boring, unless he had received news which would darken the town further.

'Our farmers' unions have contacted the church with their deepest of concerns. A new shortage of grain is ready to befall us. At this time, we must be gentle with the poor and needy, a time of austerity is upon us.'

His news was grim. A grain shortage would usually mean starvation for many. The harvest was poor in 1812, it would bring more to the gallows, who desperately tried to feed themselves.

My eyes caught the side of Isabelle, she squeezed my leg, knowing what was to come, a new uprising in the mills, starvation, pestilence, what next, I remember thinking, and then he announced, a war had been brewing within the colonies of America, it would not settle, I was beginning to feel grateful for my role as an executioner, I would not be called to defend our land, but the concern was still there.

'I shall have more jackets made, men, women, and children. Austerity is a time the hangman is at his busiest, and God's family will be as well.' Her loyalty did not waver.

'I should show my face at the chambers,' I replied. The rain had calmed. I thought it best I at least make myself known there.

'Very well.' Isabelle stepped forward. 'Just try to be home before the children are in bed. They miss you terribly.'

I kissed her forehead, hugged the children, and made my way towards the lion's Den. Roderick joined me that afternoon.

'I wonder who will be there,' Roderick asked. We hurried our way towards Hockley.

'Most likely Francis, there was a Luddite called David there the last time I frequented the place.'

'A dying breed,' chalked Roderick. I opened the door for him to step inside. 'Have you heard any more about the house?'

We ruffled the droplets of rain from our cloaks. 'They begin the build next week; we should hopefully see progress by this time next year.'

'Ah!' called Francis. His arms were wide as he hurried towards us. 'I was just talking of you.'

'I thought I felt something,' I mocked, taking his lead toward the back of the large circular room. A tall server with a tray waited by the side of the table.

'I took the liberty of ordering your drinks.' Francis sat at the table, two others sat there as well. I did not know the first, but the second I recognised and felt rather unnerved in doing so, the lord mayor of Nottingham sat beside me.

'Well, this is a wonderful surprise,' Francis snivelled. I wondered what had caused such glee. 'We were simply talking of the business of the mills.'

'A waste of time and effort,' sniggered the first man. He leant forward, reaching his hand towards me for a shake. 'Brentford, Lord Archer Brentford.'

I was not impressed by title. 'George Smith, Sir, and this is my gracious father-in-law, Roderick Dresden.'

'Of course, the engineer.' Sneered the first man. 'Lord Dutton, I must say, I have been wanting to speak with you for a while.'

Roderick raised his brows. 'Oh, well, I'm here now, though not for long, my son and I wish to return before supper, to enjoy some time with the family before normality on the morrow.'

'Yes, I shall make this quick. As an engineer, a man of industry, do you see the industry of the Luddites falling short?'

'Of course I do, textiles will eventually turn towards mechanics, people will be obsolete, when a garment can be produced at a fraction of the price it opens the market to many, the poor will no longer need to scrape in bins for a new shirt, when one can be purchased easily and cheaply, 'tis a preposterous notion to think that parliament will even get involved.'

Lord Dutton sat back, defeated by my father's knowledge.

'Although, what concerns me is the lack of mentioning to the coming hardship.'

They looked at me like I had just spat in their drinks.

'Hardship?' asked Francis.

"Twas mentioned today, in church.' I looked at their blank faces. 'You do not attend church?' They collectively shook their heads; I had never felt such shame. 'Well, they speak of the poor harvest. Austerity will hit this town, very soon.'

'Well, that's why we have you.' Lord Dutton lifted his glass to his lips. I wanted to force it into his face. I couldn't divert my eyes from his neck, checking the perfect size. 'The hangman is at his busiest during times of austerity.'

I could not do it. I knew I had to hold face. I was of the family of God and God had a plan, but it was killing me, listening to their snivelling views of poor men.

The doors burst open. We had been there less than an hour, as the watchmen arrived for a drink at the bar before taking watch in the town.

'Ah, gentlemen,' Francis stood, calling them over. 'George here tells us your duty shall soon increase.'

Their eyes searched me for answers. I leant back with my hands in my pockets, else I would throttle Francis.

'Austerity is heading towards us. With the millers' disputes, the Luddites constantly unsettled, and everything else we have to tackle. This will be a hard winter, boys.'

'It certainly will, and what with your wife expecting as well, George,' said Godfrey, stepping from the back of the others who gathered around us. 'We may need a second hangman, to see us through winter.'

'I did not know of this.' Francis was surprised by the news. I was surprised that Godfrey knew.

'Well, it won't keep me away too much. Another baby is but a blessing to create.' I hated myself for saying those words. I could feel Roderick cringing beside me. 'I know I speak of your daughter, but you've met her. The bricky lass can take care of children, while I hang others.'

My decreasing tone unnerved them. 'Yes, well, we must be to it soon, evening, Gentlemen,' bid Godfrey.

I could stand the place no longer. An insult to my wife was one thing, but the men were ungodly. They were not men of God. Passing God's judgement should never have befallen Francis Monrow.

I felt dirty quickening my pace along Smithy Row, I could feel my blood still boiling. The cold autumnal evening took my breath. Roderick did well to keep pace.

'You act, George, nothing more. This is a good thing you are doing.'

'No!' I did not mean to snap at him. I was more respectful than that. 'I cannot sit and listen to them speak of their coin filled pockets, while knowing people will starve.' A misted rain dusted my brow. 'Listening to them hurts my ears and my heart. We need a better plan, something that will see the end of those people.'

'Some are good men, George. Those are the ones you need to focus on, the ones who stand out above the others. Then you will have your plan.'

'No good man knows what happens in the place and allows it. They would have closed it by now were they good men.'

'Then what does that make us, George? Are we not good men for trying?'

'We are God's men, but they are not men of God, they are devils, and every one of them will see the righteous fury of God.'

'When their day of judgement comes, you speak dangerous words, George, you are not God, you may do his work, and I silently work beside you,' his voice snapped, 'I do it for my daughter, she loves you, George, you bring danger to your door and yet I know she wants more from you, you are one man, George, to save one life was a miracle, you have saved countless already, do not go above your station, else you will fail in God's work.'

'What if God wants me to? What if Issy was right? Making our own plan, it cannot harm us, Dad, we must do something, before the famine hits.'

He disagreed. He was silent over supper. Usually he would take to the courtyard after supper, to play with the children, but he remained melancholy by the fire. He envisioned a different retirement, and here was I, sullying his chance to spend time with his family.

'Shan't need you at the gaol this week, Dad, take a rest.'

'And when will you rest, George?' He turned on the old chair to face me. His wrinkled face had aged since he'd arrived. 'You need a break from death.'

'When God rests, as do I, times are getting harder. The people of this town need the executioner, even if they don't know it.'

'I admire your need, George, but please, think of Isabelle.'

'I think of nothing else.'

A cold bitterness was left in the room. Our relationship would have to strengthen if we were to continue God's work. With such sadness in the world, I had an additional need, a need to bring some cheer to the walls of   the   gaol.

ven the bright strips of sunlight into the court did not brighten that day. The day was a Wednesday. My ropes were lonely. It was how I liked it, but a new feeling in the room that day brought her to my eyes.

A fragile girl stepped onto the dock; her wild red hair flowed to her waist.

'Name,' called Francis.

'Peach, Sir.' Her attitude was met with an immediate rumble from the jury.

'Age.'

"Tis rude to ask a lady her age, Sir, you of all people should know that.'

A look of anger smeared across the face of Frank. She looked to be less than a teen, possibly thirteen at the latest.

'Do you know why you're here?' his lofty tone was filled with annoyance.

'Because your lawmen are wrong, they say they saw me take something, but could not find the offending item.' This girl impressed me, she was angry, she had wasted a day or more in the gaol. 'Sir, I am the daughter of a milkmaid. My time is precious, as is yours. I was taught to respect the law of this land—'

'Your grace,' the prosecution called out.

'Rude!' she interjected, 'to interrupt shows low levels of intellect and respect. I have shown this court all the respect it deserves given my treatment here.' She was a tough one. I thought Isabelle to be tough, but this girl showed promise. 'Your honour, I wish to turn your attention to the events of that night, the rain poured as I made my way along Narrow Marsh, the misting rain would've depleted the view from London Road, your so-called watchmen, could see nothing, and upon stopping me, they found nothing upon my person.'

'Then why do you believe you were arrested?' It stumped the prosecution.

She turned her head directly to Frank. 'Because, Sir, my father's property is currently being upheld by a woman, and certain men of this town believe it couth to run a single woman from her home, she refused the sale, since which we have been constantly badgered by your watchmen.'

I sat forward. The girl had a fascinating story, how true it was, was yet to be seen.

Francis swirled his eyes towards a watchman in the crowd. 'Speak.'

'Sir, we saw her fleeing toward London Road. Her hurry had us worried, and so, our Sargent ordered her immediate arrest.'

'For what?'

'Well, theft, Sir.'

'Did you find any stolen property on her person?'

He was nervous. I could smell the onset of sweat from feet away. 'No, Sir.'

'Well, in that case, Peach, you are free to leave.'

'And an apology?' Her eyes glared at the watchman.

Francis held his palm up, inviting the watchman to speak.

'I apologise, to you and yours, for the inconvenience we have caused you.'

'So you should, be weary of the milk you drink, Sir, it all comes from that farm for the town of Nottingham.'

She stormed from the dock, I crept out the side, I needed to speak to her, her rantings had caught many by surprise, none more than me.

'Excuse me,' I called to her, heading her way up High Pavement. 'Peach.' The girl stopped. Upon seeing my breathless state, she turned to face me. 'Could I have a word?'

She stepped back, weary of my being there. 'You're a lawman. I saw you in the gallery. I don't trust men of the law.'

'No, please, I am a man of the law, but I give my life to God, please, Peach, I need to know who is trying to take your land.'

My desperate plea loosened her. She turned her head, checking the street both ways.

'I suppose, we may speak, but it will be public. I do not wish to meet my maker at the hands of the law.'

I walked by her side. We headed towards the Weekday Cross, knowing the crowd would allow us to talk, without her feeling enclosed and alone.

'They started last year. My father died of a fever. My mother took over the duties of the farm, as did my brothers, but they decided to go play with the Americans.'

'They're in America?' I was concerned, but impressed. Such an undertaking showed great dedication towards our nation.

'As far as I know, the farm was left to me and my mother, until a man come knocking, said he was in the market for property, and he offered to buy the farm.' Peach walked with a flow to her steps, a poetic young girl. 'Of course, my mother would've sold, only she worried. If my brothers were to return, who would be there to greet them?'

'Do you know who he was?'

'A man called Durham, said he was searching for property, for a Lord Dunstable, of Kent. He wanted a home in the Midlands, and the farm was perfect for building. Since then, strange things have been happening.'

'Such as?'

'Such as, animals being slaughtered in the night, two calves in a week, a few of the older cows, a fox got into the coupe, the door was ajar, even though we never make such costly errors.'

'You believe it is Lord Dunstable's men?'

'If you call them that, they're devils, all of them, they say we are the lower classes, but at least we look out for each other, times are getting harder, the farm will be needed, and if this goes on, we will have no choice but to sell.'

'Thank you for your help with this, Peach. I can assure you, if those men cross my path, a short drop and a quick stop will see the end to your troubles.'

A nervous grin spread across her face. 'What's that supposed to mean?'

'Is your name really Peach?'

'No, it's Rose, and I'm not a child either. Milk soothes the ageing. I'm actually twenty-four, but being unwed, I lie about my age. Now, what is your standing in the gallery?'

'I'm the executioner.' Her skin turned pale. 'Worry not, I am not what you think I am, I kill the guilty, the innocent always slip free of my rope.'

'Well, having the executioner on side, how could I go wrong?' Her nervous laugh made me smile. I was nothing compared to the strength she had shown.

I held out my hand for a shake. 'George, and it has been a pleasure, Rose, please, if ever you need anything, I spend most of my days at the gaol.'

'Thank you, George, you have a very lucky wife.' She looked at the ring on my finger. I watched Rose disappear into the crowds of the market. Her face would stay with me for an eternity, but it was not in the way I was expecting.

Sleeping beside Isabelle, I heard a commotion outside. People were rushing through the street in the early morning mist.

A smell of smoke engulfed the air, 'twas a terrifying stench. Rushing down the stairs I bolted from the door, clambering towards St Peters Gate I found the first person in the street and grabbed her coat.

'What is it?' I called to the small, grey woman.

'Fire at the old farm of Mr Stoppard, the dairy farm.' I let her go, allowing her to rush towards the flames.

I quickly made my way to fetch my boots and cloak from the house. Isabelle called to me from the top window, 'What is it?'

'Back inside, keep the windows closed, keep the children in. I'll return as soon as I can, it's a fire at the dairy farm.'

Her face turned a pale white, the colour of milk. We both knew. I looked into her haunting brown eyes. We knew it was them who had done this to Rose.

There was nothing left of the farm. Water from the Leen was enough to extinguish the flames. A few of the cattle had survived, but the house was in ruins. Arriving at the sight, I saw Godfrey.

'Did anyone survive?' I called to him.

'Doubtful, the voluntary are checking now, but I doubt there were any survivors. We had to pry the doors open.'

My thoughts swirled. I walked towards the porch in the ruins. Something strange caught my attention. A few blackened planks of wood sprawled at the front door. I took a moment to inspect them.

Thick nails had left a mark on the doorframe. They had hammered the planks in, ensuring no one escaped.

'Evening, George,' I heard from inside the house. A local inspector came from the dull, burnt-out interior. I had mocked his appearance a few times, calling him Grim Derek, given his gaunt face looked like that of skeletal remains.

'Derek, what happened here?'

'Looks to be a stray ember from the fire. Took the mother and daughter while they slept.' He had no emotion towards the incident. 'We'll have them out by the morning. Of course, this will have to be knocked down now. Children can't stay away from places like this.'

'Although, the land now belongs to her sons.' He furrowed his brow towards me. 'Did you not know? She has two sons, currently fighting in America. They are expected to return as soon as the war is over.'

He grinned from the corner of his mouth. 'The land will be sold, and they will be paid handsomely for their profits, if they ever return that is, we are not doing well there, or in France for that matter, let us hope they return to a helpful sum, rather than a ruined farm of no value.'

There was nothing I could do. I took my knowledge and returned home. The dawn had seen Isabelle rise early. She awaited me at the table.

'They killed them, Issy. Lord Dunstable wished to have property there. Rose refused him and now she is dead. This is no coincidence.'

'I'm inclined to agree.' She looked at the old table. I could not wait to be within the warmth and comfort of our new home. 'George, I worry.' She stood to face me, taking single step by single step until she stopped at the front of me. 'I was wrong. I know what we do is God's work. There is a famine headed this way. A cloud will cover this town before winter breaks—'

Reaching forward, I held her small hands in mine. The rope was unkind to my skin, but the rough skin didn't bother her.

'Issy, we will get through this, there will be many coming to the gaol, I will let none of them slide, we will need more jackets, your hands are needed in this, as much as mine, and I will try to get more help for our cause, I cannot see you on the lane in winter, not when you're in the family way.'

'I am stronger than you often realise, but what I mean is, if they can do that to a girl and her mother, so vulnerable, if we are to be caught, then what would they do to you.'

'You said it yourself, Love, the trick is, we don't get caught.'

I know my words were not convincing to her. All I could do was hold her tight, and hope for better days to come.

Better days were far in the future. The dismal gallery that day played host to highwaymen, muggers, and thieves.

Not one of them was innocent from what I could see, but I would still speak to them all if I found the chance.

The road to Lincoln was becoming dangerous. Four highwaymen, completely unrelated, were caught along the roads. The sheriff had a new order in place, putting his men into carriages, hoping to catch the crooks before they struck an innocent.

The operation had proven to be a success to most, but to me, it showed how desperate men were becoming.

Autumn came hard that year. My rope was busier than ever, and so was God's family. I was yet to recruit another member to take on Isabelle's duties as the baby grew.

The Lion's Chambers took my time. Each day, Francis would wait for me outside the gaol. Our walk towards the chambers was often pleasant. I was falling into his trap, but my mind was still my own.

'Those rooms I asked you of?'

'No, George, your wife expects, and you speak of such things—' what I appeared to be suggesting repulsed him.

'No,' I jumped, 'I don't mean... I would never do such a thing, but something concerns me, Francis.' He stopped walking, turning towards me in the street.

'Concerns?'

'Yes, it was spoken of a while ago, a boy. I think his name was William—'

Francis held his hand up, forcing me to silence. 'I need to hear nothing more.' His tone was low. He carried secrets within his words. 'What happened was the fault of a man call Connelly, Lord Benjamin Connelly, he made a request within the chambers, his request was granted, By James Milner, the founder of the chambers, yes I am a member of the board, it was hidden from us all.' The dark streets of the town were silent. His eyes glared into mine, carrying a deadly threat. 'What I am about to tell you, remains with us.' I nodded, giving him my word. 'What he did to that boy was unfair, 'twas disgusting, the board had him thrown from the chambers, never to return, the boy on the other hand, he was put to the workhouse, where he later escaped, he would often be seen upon the street, lingering, we had to do something before he said anything, else we would all be for the gallows, the boy was given mercy, placed in God's hands.' He was delusional. I could feel his guilt.

And then I knew, Andrew Marcus Biggins. He worked at the mill, which was close to the Lace Market, a place which was close to the Lion's Chambers.

I thought hard as I sat silently in the chambers, thinking, how much Andrew knew of the Lion's Chambers, and if his knowledge had condemned him.

Returning home, I took a parchment, desperately I made my plea to the father of the church of Clifton, St Mary's. I needed Andrew to tell me all he knew of the

Lion's Chambers, and all he knew of the boy called Billy.

Days were shorter, autumn was cruel, Isabelle worked hard to save those I sent down the alley to her. Over twenty had been saved within a fortnight, more were coming. As the winter took hold, so did starvation. The town was angry.

They laughed over their drinks; hunger did not bother them in their comfort. The men of the Lion's Chambers sickened me and Roderick. He would often sit close to me, clutching my lap each time one of them spoke out of turn.

The doors opened; a tall man wandered towards the table beside ours. Leaning back in his chair, he saw our game of cards. He glared at Francis.

'I feel your eyes on me, Johnathan.'

'Then you're lucky,' said the man. He spoke down to Francis. As a judge of the town, it was something I was not expecting to see. It hindered my progress with the cards.

'While I would take your presence as a welcome distraction.' Francis turned to the man, Johnathan, 'what do you want?'

Johnathan took a large sip from his small glass. My eyes glanced between the two.

'I sent that girl to you, practically wrapped.' His muttering whisper forced Francis to lean towards him. 'And yet, my men tell me their hands were the ones to end her. I strongly advise you to do your duty. There are plenty of magistrates who would accept your place.'

My eyes flickered, wondering who he spoke of. 'She lied about her name, said it was Peach. How was I to know, plus your men had no crime for her, at least make it look convincing.' He turned in his chair, removing his eyes from the cards. 'Also, think yourself lucky I do not have George here hang you and your men for murder, such threats do not frighten me, Durham, your men are the scum in this town now, if your lord is so desperate for property, there are better ways than murder.'

I sat back, I could hardly believe what I was hearing, everything was clear, 'twas not a club for gentlemen, 'twas a place for the filthy rich to squander their wealth, buying what they wanted, what they did not get, their judge would sort out for them.

Silence hit as Johnathan left. Francis looked at the table with shame. He folded his cards. We played with check pieces. He knew my issues with gambling, but I had not lost a single game yet.

'I apologise to you, Gentlemen, Johnathan should not have spoken of such business in a place of gents.'

'Your business follows you everywhere,' I tried to reassure him. His indiscretions were all being counted by me, but I could not let him know. 'We do what we do to survive, Francis, 'tis no business of mine, whomever you send to my gallows, is not for me to question.'

'I am not a dangerous man.' Francis aged with the words he spoke, the frail judge so many feared sat as a poor old man. 'I see so much promise for this town, but that promise means we must work towards a brighter future, with the Luddites ready for another rebellion, famine heading towards us, the asylum will soon be full, and the gaol is suffering the same, we must up our game, we cannot see the gaol full during winter, too many to feed.'

'Then why not feed them on the streets?' My question unnerved him.

'We have a poor fund, they are given aide by ways of charity, the issue is not with feeding them, George, 'tis with greed, they are not content with their bread and bone soup, they wish for more, always more, and then there are the children, you are a family man, you can afford to keep your children, if you could not then you would have no more, but they breed like rabbits, unable to afford one child they go on to have six.'

His rant enraged me, everyone had a right to family, but I was a man ahead of my time, society did not see it yet, times were difficult, but it was often not the fault of the parents, as industry grew, jobs were at risk, many had been replaced by machines, the Luddites were right; they deserved the wage of skilled workers, but the future would see them completely obsolete.

The future was no longer as bright as the winter moved in. Returning that night, Roderick headed straight up the stairs towards his room. I looked at the kitchen, which was empty. I knew Isabelle's duties had taken their toll on her. Overseeing the development of the new house was exhausting, as well as growing a new life within saw her to bed early that evening.

'Twas the first time she had retired without me. A cold bowl of stew on the table was my only companion, but I was not hungry. My family was my life, but with the Lion's Chambers and gaol taking so much of my time, I could feel them slowly slipping away.

I sat at the table that night after clearing the old embers from the fire. It would be a duty less for Isabelle on the morrow, alone in the kitchen. I prayed for answers. I knew what the Lion's Chambers really were now.

Rich men could get whatever they wanted in the Lion's Chambers. Through murder, I thought to myself how many had come before, how many I had killed before, for nothing but the want of wealthy men.

I woke to a dull morning. A rattle at the door startled me. A young boy stood with a letter in hand.

'From the church, sir.' He handed the letter to me, holding his palm towards me. I placed a few coins from my pocket, seeing the glee on his face warmed the bitter morning.

Sat by the table, I read the letter, written by the hand of Father Prenton.

'*I knew the boy, William. I called him Billy. He spoke of the Stone Lion, the things they did to him. He only told me a little. It was enough to keep him away. The night they took Billy, they tried to take me, too. I ran to Fisher Gate and hid there. They saw my face, but I hoped it would never come to this. I know now, George, I'm dead, because of what they did to Billy.*

I am well though, the Father sees me well fed, I help all I can, and I've taken up more work in the stables of Sir Robert, the family have a liking to me, and it is all thanks to the family of God.'

Although his words confirmed my thoughts, I knew my family had saved him. Our duty upon this Earth was worthy. Andrew was glad in his new home, and I was glad   for   him.

Chapter Eight Far From God

Winter had seen two carts daily from the gaol, but a lot was about to change. The hangings were to be moved. My battle to remove Gallows Hill had ended. My new duty would be to hang on the hill.

A new plan would be needed. Isabelle had overseen the new property being built, as well as caring for the children and growing one. Her strength astonished me.

What I found more astonishing was her plan.

'After they're hanged, they aren't placed into the ground straight away. It could give us a chance to free them from their coffin and weigh it down, before the groundskeeper sees us.'

'It could work; however, they are all buried before nightfall. The cover of darkness would help,' Roderick interjected.

'I may have an idea for that.' I remembered a while ago, talks in the Lion's Chambers of proper burial rites.

'There's been talk lately, saying that a proper burial, even for those of criminal convictions, should take place with proper mourning, they are suggesting a night in the chapel of rest before burial the next day, perhaps we need to encourage this?' I looked at Roderick; I could see he held the same thought as me.

The day was a Saturday. We would rarely visit the Lion's Chambers at a weekend, but our need was great.

'Well, don't be out too late, both of you. I have a surprise when you return, so please, be back before the hour is too late.'

I don't know what she meant by that, but myself and Roderick could feel a new plan forming. Those we had saved were worthy, but so many had hit the gallows since, we needed to strengthen God's family to ensure we could continue his work.

The Chambers were quiet as we entered. Our usual table, around the corner and towards the back, held its usual occupant. Francis sat alone.

His face beamed as we walked towards him. A steward took my cloak. A drink was soon upon the table before we had even sat.

'Tis strange to see you here,' mentioned Francis. He reached to a small box in the wall at the side of the table, taking out the deck of cards.

'I thought you may be able to use the company.' I sat beside Roderick. He took the checks pieces from the box, but before he placed them down, I reached over. 'Shall we play for proper coin?'

His eyes crossed to Roderick, who appeared all too concerned. 'You're sure?'

I knew I needed to up my game and gain a better standing in the chambers. Manipulation was not something I was good at, but if I wanted my way with Gallows Hill, I knew I would need to do something.

'I believe he will do well.' Roderick looked pridefully towards me. 'Set an allowance. When you're through, we move to the checks.'

'Agreed,' said Francis. He was no longer the bitter judge I so despised. He was used by the others there. I would've felt pity for him, but he had allowed them to use him for so long.

'So, Gallows Hill,' I mentioned, handing out the cards for our first game. His eyes drifted towards me. He was doubtful it would be a pleasant conversation. 'I ask you for very little, Francis, but there is one thing I will ask, and that is for you to listen.'

'I always listen to you, George, I know I press fun on you, but you're a man I will always respect.'

'And I you, and that is why I come with a warning for you.' His eyes flickered as he looked at his cards. Roderick looked confused, knowing I would rarely play with coin. 'The people of the town talk. I visited the Weekday Cross this Wednesday, where I heard fearful whispers. They are concerned that improper burial rites will see the town flooded with ghosts of criminals.' I smirked at him. He was not a man of superstition. He believed it to be a sign of low intellect.

'I know your feelings towards this, Francis, however, if those upon the streets of this town feel some great wrong is being committed, at the moment they wish for any excuse for a riot.'

'Perhaps you're right.' His eyes did not leave the cards, not even for a glance. 'I can speak with the groundsman, see what he suggests. However, the hangings must be placed back into the eyes of the public. This is why so many are coming through now.' His argument was invalid, but he would never see it that way. 'They do not see the consequences of such callous acts of villainy, so they feel free to commit such acts, George, I do believe I fold.'

He huffed as he threw his cards down. I had indeed won. Which gave me a worthy idea.

Upon leaving the Chambers, I had gained myself a healthy twenty guineas, almost a year's wage for most within the town.

'You played well this evening, George.'

'I did, which gives way to another idea,' I replied with glee. I liked my plan, but Roderick did not appear so taken. 'Upon saving these people, what happens to them? I often wonder, they live as paupers, we give them a second chance at life, but what of a second chance of living?' He looked at me, as though I spoke like a madman. 'What I mean is, we should drain them, every last shilling, everything they have, and give to those we save, to make for a healthy living for them, else we are sending them towards a slower death.'

'I understand your thinking, George, and I admire your concern. However, we already place ourselves at significant risk. Gambling will place us at further risk.'

I opened the door for Roderick to step through. He froze as he looked into the kitchen.

Stepping in, I saw the reason why. Isabelle had her father's feminine looks, whereas her brother, Joseph, he had the looks of his mother. He stood dishevelled in the kitchen, an awkward silence hit.

'Father,' he said with a quivering voice, stepping forward. Roderick walked past him, shunning the hand he held out to him.

'Joseph,' I greeted, seeing how awkward it was for him, I could not leave the poor man in such a state. I shook the hand he held out. 'What brings you out here?'

'My duty.' Joseph's eyes remained with his father. An uncomfortable silence from Roderick chilled the air. 'I was in Ireland. Upon hearing of mother, I had to return. I had no word. I found out through Aunt Ellen.'

'If I knew where you were, I could've told you,' snapped Roderick. The children remained in the courtyard at the back. 'Probably wasting your life on some ship.'

'Father, I was with the navy, doing my duty.'

'Then return to your duty.' His mouth curled with such hate and anger, 'twas something I had not seen in Roderick before, usually such a placid man. He had me shocked.

'I can't return. I owe a debt here, to you, and I am here to try and repay that debt, if you would only let me.'

'I do not wish for your coin, boy.'

'Then, perhaps he could repay another way.' Isabelle stepped forward, placing her hand on her brother's shoulder. 'Perhaps, the family of God could use a new member?'

She trusted him. I could see it, but I knew his crime. 'He stole from me, Isabelle. Such a duty can only be with trusted men, and I struggle to trust him,' spat Roderick. His snapping unnerved me.

'I stole little from you, Father.'

His arguing would not win him any respect from his father, nor his ear.

"Tis not what you stole, Joseph, the fact you stole it, that is what pains me, that is what tore your mother apart.'

'Then let me repay you in kind, please, I cannot return, so I wish to repay the respect I owe you.'

'This could work,' I stepped forward. With my words in his head, Roderick calmed. 'This family is a family of second chances, Dad.' As I said that word, 'dad,' Joseph flickered his hurt eyes. 'What kind of family are we if we do not give second chances to our own blood?'

'He's right, father, please, Joseph has a place in the town, he can help us with our endeavour.'

Roderick pointed at Joseph and spoke to Isabelle, 'How much does he know?'

'Nothing yet, I was awaiting your return.'

'Chances, Roderick,' I warned, seeing his trust in Joseph waver. 'He has been away for a long time, he has fought for our nation, we owe it to him, to pay our respects to his service.'

'Well, I suppose it is good to see you again.' Roderick broke, he had missed his son, I could see a dew forming in his eye, but before his tears would break, he sat at the table, offering Joseph a seat beside him.

Isabelle made a wonderful roast that evening. The children were beyond excited to see the uncle they had forgotten. They flooded him with questions, and I did not hold them back, as I wondered the same myself.

'I was very little upon the ship. The kitchens saw me busy for the day. A cook is all I was. I saw the world from the stove.' He held back, not wanting to tell us the truth.

'And what of the war?' I asked, gaining an interest.

'The ports are always alive with talk, but a drunken sailor at a port is less than reliable information, I never drifted beyond there, when we landed in Portsmouth last month, I found myself in trouble upon one of the ships, so I returned here, handing in my papers, now all I need is a job.'

'Digger?' I looked at Roderick, who laughed at the suggestion. It lost Joseph with the humour.

'We have been on a mission, for over a year now,' Isabelle was awkward, her words stuttered. 'You see, George, he is the town — Well, he—'

'I'm the town executioner.' I no longer held shame in my duty. 'Your father has become my assist, however, those who hang don't always deserve it. My duty has grown from executioner to saviour.'

'I don't understand.'

'This town is corrupt, Joseph. It keeps me and your father busy, trying to find those who deserve to hang, and those who do not. Over a hundred lives have been saved by us so far.'

'A hundred?' His gasp concerned me. 'In just a year, a hundred people would've been hanged? They don't even have that many in London. Sounds like it's a town of villains.'

'That's the problem though, uncle.' The bitterness in Geoffrey's voice hit me. 'I had a friend once, who hanged at the gaol, for playing a game of seek, they hang you for anything around here, one of the scullery maids from Wollaton Hall, she was hanged for speaking out of turn and being too loud at market, says she was too crude for society, of course she was one of the saved, but she never should have been there in the first place.'

'They are out of control, and our mission changes daily. We are with a new mission now, one we are yet to reveal to all of you. We are to drain them of their funds.' I looked at Isabelle, knowing her concern grew with each word I spoke. 'I was a gambling man once, but now, my gambling will see these people go free and live a life they deserve, away from poverty and cruelty.'

'How is it done?' asked Joseph, knowing a public hanging was hard to achieve if we left the victim alive.

'I'm the hangman, Joe, but you sit with the family of God, so far he has willed it, the victims of the rope are told all they need to do, I give them lessons before the hanging, and then we rescue them from their graves before they bury them, taking them to the church in the village of Clifton, from there they are free.'

'But why so many?'

'Because our good judge and his friends of the Lion's Chambers wish to see this town free from poverty, they take what they want, leaving a trail of destruction in their wake, death follows them, they are dangerous, their need to bring industry to this town is frightening, they insist

upon a higher society in Nottingham, leaving the poor
and needy at the gallows.'

'So, unless you have a healthy wage, your life is at risk.'

'Exactly that. The town is constantly growing. It would
be a good thing, but they build on the bodies of the
poor.' My hate for those in the Lion's Chambers had
grown, but I could do nothing but drain them of their
funds and save all those who needed saving.

The family retired that night, Joseph took a place on
our sofa. Isabelle and I found comfort in each other's
arms in our bed.

'I cannot see you gamble our lives away, George,' said
Isabelle as she sat upright in bed.

'We need funds, otherwise, we save them, only to see
them towards a life of poverty.'

'There is another way.' She looked over her shoulder
at me. 'They gamble with lives, but property is what they
truly desire.'

'You are suggesting investment?' I asked, Isabelle
nodded. 'We have no property big enough for them to
invest in.'

'Who says we need property? These men gamble, and
the house always wins. If they are convinced enough,
they will invest in an idea.'

The gaol was busy that day. Moans and groans had turned to screaming and shouting. I could see cold in the air from every cell as their breath misted through the bars.

I had chosen those I could save that day; the highwaymen and robbers would see my rope upon Gallows Hill, but those who had stolen to feed their family, those who had made the mistake of being poor, I would spare them my rope.

Gallows Hill would be busy that day. I would have to work fast, ensuring that the worthy placed their jackets on before leaving the gaol, Roderick and I took the condemned towards the hill.

A small pub on the way towards the gallows would see the condemned relax before the rope. Having so many on the cart, we opted to remain outside, Roderick called into the pub. The landlord of the Nag's Head brought our beverages to us.

The first man wandered towards the gallows. He was one of the guilty. His hanging would help the innocent see the proper way to die. We had ten that day, we would save six, they would bury four in the marshes.

I tried to ensure a guilty man would be left, as they had a nasty habit of leaving a body to hang overnight, warning the newcomers to the town, crimes would be punished with death.

The day was busy; the night was bitter, but God's family began their evening shift within the graveyard at the marshes. Silently we worked, removing their jackets, and seeing them in Roderick's carriage. It would be the duty of Joseph to take them to the church in the village.

The ghosts of Broad Marshes watched us that night. Strange figures of graves unnerved us as we worked silently. Beyond the wall, a moving shadow forced us all down. I knew it that the watchmen would often pass the marshes on their way towards London Road.

Our work completed, the hour was past midnight before we arrived back, I could see the struggle my family had suffered, Isabelle held her back, her belly was now wide with child, it exhausted the children, their lessons for the next day would have to wait until the afternoon, my family was suffering, but God's cause was much greater than our suffering.

They led twelve people towards Gallows Hill. Isabelle stood on the path beside Joe. The children remained in Joseph's carriage; I did not wish for them to see what their father's hand was capable of.

I would save ten that day, the jackets were working, but the fear of failure was always there, these were nothing but poor men and woman, a man accused of poaching for fish along the Leen, 'twas no crime, 'twas hunger.

The busy weeks of austerity continued to dampen our nights, I had not seen the Lion's Chambers in far too long, I hoped for a day of rest, the church on Sunday saw us all exhausted, the children would often fall to sleep, being forced awake by myself or Isabelle.

With only a few months left, we needed to be ready for the new arrival. The overseeing of the new home was almost complete. It had taken less than a year to build, with a new child on the way. We would need the space, but what Isabelle had created, I was yet to see.

The move was set for the first day in December. Having us settled in the home before Mass brought great excitement to us all. Joseph had done well, although I could tell he was suffering.

'I'm a man, George. Living off my sister's husband is hardly what a man should be doing. I need employment.'

'As Francis would say, poppycock.'

'Who's Francis?' Joseph helped with the last few trunks from the cart. The home in front of us was a gargantuan beast compared to where we had come from. Large windows spewed light into all the airy rooms. The kitchen separated from the dining room, a large parlour room with a tall fire. It was magnificent what Isabelle had achieved.

'Francis is the man you might meet at the gaol, why not join me later next week, I'm sure they always need gaolers and foremen, you would fit into the place well.'

'Does it pay?' Money was his only concern.

'It pays well enough.' I helped him with the large trunk, carrying it in backwards. 'Besides, I would not see my brother-in-law above the spindly shops, unless of course you have Bromley manor in mind.'

'Hind's Yard is not that bad.'

'Come on, Joe, we all know the mansion hides a lot in Hind's Yard, even if you have seen the goings on there, you'd be brave to speak of it, I'm the town executioner, and your sister is one of the best gossips this town has ever known, I know as much as the cobbles below us.'

He smiled at my posturing. 'Do you think they would take me on at the gaol?'

'Why wouldn't they, you're a navy man, a man of excellent reputation, you're certainly no criminal.' We struggled up the few steps of the house. 'I shall take you Wednesday, to the Lion, seeing Francis will better your chances, plus, a few of the watchmen are usually there, they'll know of well-paid work in the area.'

'I would rather remain in or near the gaol, I may even go for the new sheriff's post.'

I gave a hearty laugh. Joseph was a man of kind words. He could convince a donkey 'twas a horse. 'I would only wish to see that day, Joe.'

'Father!' I heard Bethany call to me, running from the room at the side of the front door. Her excitement had taken hold of her. 'Daddy, this place is wonderful.'

We both struggled with the chest. Having Bethany rushing past us did not help.

'Bethany, go to your mother, we're busy,' snapped Joseph, I did not take it lightly him snapping at her like that, but he was right, we were busy, and 'twas dangerous to have her running through the halls.

'Do as he says, Beth, to your mother.'

'You really should have a tighter leash upon the children, George, especially in an area such as this one. Children should never be heard, and they should never be out of place, not with this society.'

It cut like a knife to hear Joseph say such things. 'I have ample control over them. I simply see it as unfair to cut a child from the ways of nature at such an innocent age, it's excitement, Joe, and I am glad they can show it.'

'You're a patient man, George. I would've seen the belt to them long ago,' he laughed as though he was mocking. I did not find the amusement in his statement.

With the house settled, I took Joseph upon the Wednesday to meet with Francis. I had told Francis I would bring a guest that evening, explaining that

Isabelle's brother, a man of the royal navy, had moved back into the town.

Francis showed little excitement when I spoke to him within the court, but as we walked into the Chambers, a different mood had hit him. A small quartet in the corner of the chambers warmed the air with music.

'George, and this must be Joseph.'

'Please, Sir, call me Joe.'

'Well, Joe, what'll it be?'

'I will join you in whatever you're having.'

'Certainly.' Francis lifted his hand to the steward. 'Tell me, what brings you back to Nottingham?'

'Industry,' Joseph's reply was immediate. 'I've seen the potential of this town, and investment now would see a promising return in the future.'

'Ah, so you have an investment in mind?'

'Not yet.' He narrowed his eyes towards Francis. 'I was rather hoping to become better acquainted first, and as you know, where better to find the truth of a town than within the local gaol?'

'I like your thinking.' Francis leant forward, reaching to the wall. He took the box of cards. It would be another chance to drain him of more coin.

'My thinking is to become better acquainted with the law. Remaining on the correct side of it, was something I always planned. However, seeing the town from a different viewpoint will see my investment grow further.'

'So, I suppose what he is asking, Francis, is there anything you can do, to allow him footing within the town.'

'You make it sound so crude, George,' Joseph gave a shying laugh.

'Not at all. He simply understands my need for honesty. Besides, my age is no longer on my side. I feel it hourly. Quickening conversation is what I often need. I can find you something within the law to see your investment well within this town, your right, we are a growing town, and this is the building it all grows from.'

A sneering grin disturbed me, but he was right. That was the building the town was growing from, through greed and corruption.

Joseph did well with his meeting with Francis. We walked back through the cold streets. The works along Cow Lane were finally completed. Having changed its name to Clumber Street long ago, I still struggled to refer to it as such.

Every corner we turned offered more views of a growing industry within the town. The gas lights brightened the streets, allowing the silent half-built structures to be gazed upon by me and Joseph.

'You did well in there,' I complimented him through gritted teeth. The cold had caused a great pain within our backs, my jaw clenched shut, my teeth had done with clattering, 'twas far too cold.

'I know how to talk to these men; the ships are crawling with them.'

'The navy men?'

'Navy men are nowt but liars, most of their reputations are built upon lies, George, it was the one thing I learnt, even if you have nothing, make it appear you have something, and they will go out of their way to help your progress.'

'So the investment, then?'

'What investment? I have nothing, George, I left the ship as a poor man, discharged for my need to gamble, I only made it here through the kindness of strangers, who offered a lift to the navy man, I talk my way through life, George, seems to be the only thing I'm good at.'

'I don't believe that, Joe, you're a good man, with your heart in the right place, you'll go far in this world, and in this town, hard work and dedication will get us there.'

'Well, you're the executioner. I'm certainly not going to argue with you.'

The stunning sight of home came into view. The gate to the house was small but spectacular. Every bit of that place was home, but what made it better than I ever believed I deserved was the greeting from my wife and children. Each day, upon my return, they would be there, waiting for a warm embrace.

The family of God was the family of Smith. I never believed I could be so lucky. With the wide, bright fire roaring in the sitting room, I sat with Isabelle. Roderick and Joseph remained in the dining hall, trying to better their differences.

My family was together. For once, the hangman was glad to be in the dismal town.

'I have a plan,' announced Joseph as he stood. 'Those men are interested in investment.'

Roderick stood. 'When I first arrived, I planted a seed in the minds of those in the chambers, investment into the waterways.'

'I may not be good at gambling, but if I can convince them to invest in a company which does not exist, we can free people with plenty to restart their lives.'

'And when they see no company exists?'

Asked Isabelle.

'It will exist, a new works is in the process of building. If it reaches a point where their investment is seen as false, I've disappeared before, I can do it again.'

Isabelle stood, rushing to her brother. 'It's too dangerous.'

He smirked. 'I fought the seas, Issy, it's beyond dangerous, but these men, when they have nothing left, they will have no one to find me, let me do this, let me help you.'

I knew she did not want to discuss it further. I could feel her eyes on me all night, wondering what I thought. I knew it would get him killed if he were to be found out, but we played a dangerous game as well. Whatever he had planned, I would not be the man to get in his way.

Neither Isabelle nor I had any reason to doubt our plan now. Gallows Hill was busier than ever, taking the condemned during the bitterness of a dead winter, to be hanged upon the hill.

The worsening weather had seen many toward starvation. Highwaymen were the worst they had ever been. The road to Lincoln was an area of ill repute now, a place few would travel alone at night.

Pepper Street had seen a new trade. Ladies of the night had taken to the area. The town was dragged down further by those from Fisher Gate, who would use the brothels for their own needs.

Several women had been through Gallows Hill. They each walked free, with a pocket of coin from the judge himself, 'twas not their fault they would have to sell their dignity to feed a starving family.

The winter made us all rejoice at the sight of Isabelle and her growing self. The excitement of the children to receive a new sibling was clear, and we were beyond excited.

Joseph and Roderick were on better terms. Roderick had even paid Joseph's access fees for the Lion's Chambers, allowing him year-round access.

The world was looking brighter, Gallows Hill was quietening. Upon reaching ten on some days, the hangings slowed. We had only four that day. It would see us within the Lion's Chambers well before we would be suspected of any mischief.

Having sent them on their way, we walked side by side up the lane. Isabelle remained with the children. We remained at the back, watching our little loves bounce along the road.

Bethany froze along Low Pavement. Turning to the right, she was unable to breathe.

'Bethany,' Isabelle called out. Her motionless stare worried us all. We quickened towards her.

Arriving at Low Pavement, several of the sheriff's men made their way towards her. Upon seeing me there, they slowed their pace.

'George,' called Godfrey, 'what has you all out here?'

'The children wished to see the Leen.'

He laughed at my comment. 'All you'll catch in the Leen is a floating turd and a fever.'

'Due north, it's cleaner at the Trent, of course they didn't go far, just a few ducks to feed after a day of hanging,' I mocked. Walking closer towards him, I placed my hand on his shoulder, forcing him down, putting him in his place. 'I hope to see you at the Lion later. Joe, Roderick and I will spend a night bleeding the judge of funds.'

'I bet you will,' his snivelling tone caught me. I did not like the man, he could tell. I was dreadfully poor at hiding it.

'We may be by later, but for this evening, I bid you all well. Men of the law must always be watchful for mischief.'

'Absolutely. I hope for a busy day tomorrow as well. Austerity pays well.' I could give nothing but a smirk as he passed by us with his henchmen in tow.

We made our way back to the house with Isabelle and the children. We would not allow them to walk alone. We had seen far too much from crooks and thieves.

The Lion was quiet that evening, a crackling fire, and soft music invited us in, the voice of Rose sang blissfully in the background.

Francis was in his usual place; a drink was already in his greying hand.

'Evening, Francis,' I greeted as I sat, holding my hand to the steward. He was ready with a drink before I had sat.

'It's a quiet evening, glad to see you're here,' his grumbling tone spoke of a deep depression.

'We were planning on draining you of coin this evening, but I assume you are in no fit state for such things.'

'You know me too well, George.'

The evening was pleasant, even with the odd few slamming doors from the upper balcony, I knew what was in those rooms, but I had drowned out the atrocities, I would save them upon my rope, I could do nothing within the Lion.

A swirling draught hit me. Looking at the door, Godfrey and his men rushed in. Sheriff Williams met them at the door.

'Empty?' I heard him blurt, 'well then we have body snatching, check the asylum, the hospitals.'

I held my head low, seeing him quickly walking towards us.

'My lord,' he looked at Francis.

'I have warned you before, Henry, 'tis Francis here.'

'Very well, Francis, we have a problem.' Francis lifted his head to listen. 'My men are reporting issues within the Marshes. They say that body snatchers may be on the prowl.'

Francis raised his brows at me. 'We are in times of great austerity,' I said as I turned to Henry. 'We were that way earlier, but saw nothing in the Marshes. However, it is possible, whoever did this, were simply after clothes.' I did not want to give myself away. I needed to be surprised with news of a missing corpse.

'And what use would they have of a body?' his tone was snapping, unhappy with my reply.

I sighed, turning to Roderick. 'Where was it, I recall a press paper, a while ago, telling of a village so far down on its luck?' — I narrowed my eyes towards him, — 'that one where they were forced to feast on their dead to survive.'

'That is singularly the most disgusting thing you have ever said,' moaned Francis.

'I highly doubt the people of this town are consuming the dead, George,' argued Henry. 'Besides, surely we would've seen something. Are you sure they were dead after today's hanging?'

I abruptly stood, giving a hard face toward Henry. 'I do not take lightly to such questions. I do a thorough job. No one survives my rope, not even you would, so, yes, they were dead before boxed.'

He took a step back, relaxing his eyes. 'I simply have to ask.'

'Henry, offer a handsome reward to any with information, offer more than what a body is worth, and someone will come forward, possibly even the culprit themselves, hoping to finger an innocent to claim his own reward.'

'Well, how much are you suggesting?'

'Twenty guineas, should keep them interested, for each man who is brought to justice, George, you should be more rattled with this, they're your right to sell.'

'It always made me wonder why you never did.' Henry glared at me.

I gave little thought to my reply. 'I am a man of God, we are all equal in God's garden, as such, I have no right to a dead man, we are God's children, he will see fit what happens to them.'

'You're a strange one, George,' commented Henry. He turned to leave. 'Likable, but strange.'

They were not men of God; they would never understand the sanctity of death. Francis was appointed his duty through education and belief, a belief of God, but they had corrupted God, every one of them.

I felt my blood run cold, for such an amount many would willingly line the Marshes, hoping to find a chance at making twenty guineas. Our plan would again need to change.

Upon returning to the house, we were met with emptiness, lighting some of the gas lamps. I checked the house was clear. Joseph and Roderick retired.

Making my way up the stairs, I heard a moan from Bethany's room. Not wanting her to wake her mother, I ventured in with a lamp in hand.

'Father.' She rubbed her eyes as she sat up in her bed, 'twas much more comfortable for her now. I had provided for my family, the greatest gift any man could receive.

'What is it?' I whispered, not wanting to wake her sleeping brother in the other room.

'I had a bad dream.' Her glistening eyes looked at me; I should have listened to her. 'Some wicked men, Daddy, they came for us, they broke the door, and took you and Mummy away.'

Stroking her hair, I shushed her. There was something remarkable with Bethany. I loved my children, but something strange in her often caught me off guard.

'That will not happen, you're safe here, I swear to you.'

She laid back down peacefully in her bed. My words consoled her.

I could not sleep that night, the rushing wind outside our window kept me awake, but worse was the knowledge that my family would again be forced to think of another plan, to remove the saved from their resting place, else they would suffer worse than the rope.

There had not been a live burial for an age in the town, however, most still insisted on being buried with a vial of poison, just in case they woke within a world of darkness. It was still kinder than the rope.

The morning broke quickly for me. A calling of birdsong close to the woodland behind our new kingdom spoke of a better world to come.

The bells of St Peters chimed far in the distance; I could barely make out their dulling moans.

I heard her as she struggled out of bed. 'Issy.' I quickly rose from the bed, attempting to help her up.

'I am fine, George,' she sniggered, 'I am with child, not death, not yet at least.'

Her mocking fell hard on me that day. 'I have something I need to tell you; they discovered the empty coffins; they are now offering twenty guineas to anyone who can bring the snatchers to justice.'

'Twenty?' her lofty tone of surprise was expected; 'twas a high price to pay. 'Oh, George, how can we do this now? They will fill the Marshes on watch. I have no other way.'

'Back to the gaol.' A small voice behind me shocked us both. Geoffrey stood behind us, ready to help his mother from the bed. He placed his arms out, helping her to stand. He was not only a man now, but he was also a gentleman.

'Surely the judge will see sense in moving the hangings back to the gaol, until the snatchers move to the next county at least.' His grin warmed me.

'I have an idea,' said Isabelle, 'I need to go to the Weekday today, so I can pay a special visit to Francis at the gaol, perhaps if he hears it from me, it will ease him into agreeing.' I shuddered at the thought of seeing her inside that place.

Geoffrey soon perked up, 'You can take some of the bread we made, the one with lavender, I think he would like that.'

Here they stood, my family, the family so dedicated to God, they were willing to walk into the pits of hell, just to see our duty upon this earth fulfilled.

'I can't have you in there, it would cause unrest.'

'You are a man of great prowess.' She leant up; pride shone in her eyes. 'You can do as you please, even taking your wife to meet your colleague.'

'Colleague? he is the man who practically owns me.'

'And yet, you still live by your own law.'

Her lavender bread certainly would be a treat, not only for the gaolers, but also for Francis. He was not used to such home delights, having no wife to cook for him, he would be treated to the more upmarket of culinary pleasures, but nothing compared to lumpy lavender bread.

Knocking on the door of his chambers, I looked at her excited face. I did not expect Francis to be as excited.

'Enter,' he called from within.

Stepping in, his smile grew. Upon seeing my wife, it withered.

'My lord,' she greeted with open arms, it caused a stir with Francis. 'I have heard so much about you, and I am yet to meet the man of such prowess.'

He fiddled with his collar, readying himself for a day of court.

'You must be Isabelle?'

'Please, Issy, I feel like I know you, you're all George talks about, he admires you greatly, and in doing so, as do I.'

Her smile alone lightened him; I saw his glum face turn to a look of glee. 'Well, what has you in a place as awful as this?'

'You do, of course.' She gave a light snigger, looking back at me and Francis. 'I was heading towards the Weekday this morning, and I could hold myself no longer. I decided to bring you a little home comfort. You do so much for our town. I'm surprised you are not constantly rewarded.'

She looked around his glum chambers. Nothing but a few papers upon his ink-stained desk, bookshelves lined the walls, all contained books of complicated law.

She passed the bread to Francis, wrapped in a thin cloth. 'Our son, he insisted we bring you some lavender bread. Upon hearing of my plans to visit, he also admires you.'

'Ah, what a pleasure,' I saw him age before me. The sullen look of ill temperament died from his withering face, an age in his youth returned. Isabelle had worked a miracle with the judge.

'Please, have a seat, I see you're in the way of family.' He pulled a chair out, ready for her to sit.

'I would not wish to burden you; besides, you have a busy day ahead, ridding our streets of the unwanted,' she mocked, even Francis thought it amusing.

'Well, perhaps you could come by later, at around twelve, myself and George will retire for a while, we could fetch our lunch together.'

She gave a tight smile, straightening her back. 'I have a better idea. Would you dine with us, this evening? I have word of a fine cut of venison fresh at the butchers on Fleshers this morning. I have a promise he would save the best cut for me.'

'That sounds like the most wonderful evening,' he was childlike in his reply.

'Return this evening with George. I shall have the children bathed and in bed before you arrive.' Her promise warmed him more.

'I can hardly wait.'

She had rubbed off on Francis. Her effervescence had woken the child in him.

'I do believe this will be a short day.'

My miracle of a wife had lulled the judge, so much so, not one person was sentenced that day, he even pardoned one man who cried upon the stand, claiming, 'No man of guilt would show such remorse, even to save his own life.'

As the day ended, my duty within the gaol was done. I felt an emptiness within my gut, a feeling of loss deep inside. The evening with Francis would need to be perfect, else he would never return, we did not need him on side, we simply needed to sway him, moving the hangings back to the gaol, until the business of body snatchers was through.

'Gentlemen,' greeted Isabelle, as we stepped into the wide hall. She took Francis's cloak, dusting off the small droplets of rain which had hindered our return.

'A pleasure to see you again, Issy.' He became a child again. His look towards Isabelle was nothing like the man I had seen before.

'Daddy,' I heard Bethany at the bottom of the stairs.

'I apologise,' sighed Isabelle, wide eyed. 'I tried to get them into bed, but of course they refused to sleep without first saying goodnight to their father.' I could see Geoffrey behind her. Both were ready for bed, and I knew Isabelle had planned it.

'Good night.' I kissed Bethany's forehead and ruffled Geoffrey's hair. 'I shall see you bright and early on the morrow, quiet now, we have an esteemed guest.'

A mystery in my eyes forced them both to look. Geoffrey gasped with glee. 'Good evening, Lord.'

Francis bowed towards him. 'And goodnight.' His smile was tight and wide. I used to think he did not like children, but Isabelle instantly changed that for him.

Retiring into the dining room, Francis looked elated. 'Something smells delightful.'

'Venison, just as promised.' Her wide smile met him; Roderick followed from the kitchen, carrying a tray. Joseph was not far behind him, he too helped Isabelle with the table.

The meal was delightful. Isabelle was always a wonderful cook, but she had gone beyond, and it impressed the judge remarkably well.

Leaning back with a full belly, Isabelle reached towards a bottle on the dresser.

'I would retire to leave you gentlemen, but this is far too much fun.' She began pouring drinks for us. She chose not to partake that evening.

'Oh, please, Issy, stay, you lighten the room,' insisted Francis. It was odd for a woman to join us for drinks, but Francis insisted.

Dreary talk soon led to talk of the gaol, and Isabelle found the perfect moment.

'I say, I saw notice this afternoon, posted in the window of Bridle Smith Gate, telling of some awful business of grave robbers.'

'Such talk should not dampen our evening,' said Francis.

'Not dampening at all.' Joseph soon turned the conversation back, 'Issy is a wonder with town speaking.' His mockery was indeed true.

'You stop,' she joked, 'but it is true, they blessed me with a gift to talk the harp from an angel.' Francis laughed; she intrigued him. 'However, I heard talk.' She quickly looked at Francis. 'Which was passed directly to Henry. The Luddites are not pleased with John Leavers. The man has turned a new machine, making lace easier to make. They say he will soon move in on them.'

'Bloody Luddites are all I hear of at the moment,' complained Francis. Leaning back, he took a sip from his glass. Isabelle leant over, filling his glass.

'Well then, I also heard a woman on Beast Hill speaking of the atrocities of the graves. She was saying no one is pleased to hear such news, that the law should be doing better than asking for rewards.'

'What do they expect from us?'

'Well, from what I could hear, they would rather the executions be moved back to the gaol, giving the family of the deceased ample time to prepare a watch over the grave, this is of course if the conviction allows for a burial.'

'Of course it will. George has only ever sold a few to the surgeons, it is something he still chooses not to do.'

'I am still in the room.' I sat forward, receiving a warm smile from Isabelle.

'I believe it would be best to move them back to the gaol,' Roderick finally spoke. He had been quiet that evening.

'What good would it do?' sighed Francis. 'A condemned man would only rot within the ground. If someone makes a few extra guineas from his suffering, it can only help in the advances of the living.'

'You've spoken to far too many surgeons,' said Isabelle with a spark of laughter. 'I cannot but agree that it helps science, but condemned or not, their bodies are their property still. No man has a right to take it. Think of it this way, would you wish for your grave to be disturbed, for your body to be defiled in such a way, condemned or not, we must stop all atrocities in Nottingham, else the body snatchers will see our town as an easy target.'

'We need to deter them, perhaps a pack of dogs within the cemetery might help,' snickered Francis, 'I agree, I shall see to the hall on the morrow, see if we can move the executions back to the gaol, just until the spate has ended.'

The conversation became light. Usually, Francis would be in the Lion's Chambers until ten. The hour was almost past midnight before he gave a final stretch.

'I regret to inform you; I must be going.'

'Tomorrow is Saturday, why not remain here this evening, it would be a crime to see a judge on the street at this hour,' laughed Isabelle, her hospitality had gone beyond.

'My dear, you have gone above and beyond, George. You are an incredibly lucky man.' I smiled and nodded;

I knew how lucky I was. 'However, I am required at the hall in the afternoon, I must be on my way.'

'Joe, the carriage,' insisted Isabelle. Joseph slumped in his chair. We all felt the hour hit hard.

'Of course,' Joseph stood, making his way from the house as he readied the horse at the stables at the bottom of the yard outside.

Isabelle readied Francis's cloak. 'Please, we must make this regular.'

'I would be honoured.' Francis's gleeful reply sparked a smile from Isabelle.

'We could make it each Friday, from the gaol, but next week, I insist, you must stay. If you think dinner is a treat, you're yet to sample breakfast.'

Her tight smile warmed him again. He looked giddy after meeting Isabelle. Her warmth had thawed the cold heart of judge Francis Monrow.

Seeing him in the carriage, he waved at Isabelle and Roderick, who remained at the door.

Placing a foot on the step, he asked, 'Will I be seeing you at the Lion this weekend?'

'Of course, Issy always insists we take church on Sunday, but we will all join you after I return Issy and the children home.'

'I shall see you Sunday then.' He leant his head from the window of the carriage. 'I must say, George, I do envy you. Your family is beautiful. If I had been blessed with such a thing, who knows, I might not have become the callous man I am today.' His mocking caught me off guard.

'You're warmer than you believe, Francis, safe journey,' I bid him, stepping from the carriage I watched as it rode down the lane.

I was brimming as I stepped back inside. 'Issy, you are a marvel.'

'I am exhausted,' she gave a hearty laugh. 'I hope it worked.'

'Well, if not, we try him again next Friday.' I raised my brows at her.

'Oh, come on, George, we have to keep him on side. If ever we get caught, he will be our only hope. He already likes you, now I believe he likes me too.'

'Likes? He is infatuated, but so am I.' I took her by the hand, kissing the back. 'He was very right with one thing, I am the luckiest man to ever grace this Earth, to have a wife as beautiful, as dedicated, and as perfect as you, I don't know where you get the energy, and I don't know what I did to deserve you, but I am glad I did.'

A tear caught her delicate brown eyes, 'You are a man deserving of the best, George, from the moment you jumped me, I saw the dedication you had, a dedication you deserved in turn, now, to bed, you will be waking with the children on the morrow, I need my rest.'

'Only a few weeks, and he will be here.'

'He?'

'Well, you're carrying low, tells me a boy is on the way.'

'I carried low with Bethany, and high with Geoffrey.'

'Well, if I were a betting man.' She scowled at me. 'If I were, I would bet for a boy to see us into the next year.'

'I have awhile yet, George, and now with everything being back to the gaol, Joe will be an invaluable asset.' She turned on the stairs, facing me directly. 'Although, I still wish to be there for them, when they arrive at the lane, I still want to be there to see them, to help them.'

'Of course, God's family would be nothing without Isabelle Smith, the cheerful face of an angel there to greet them upon their arrival toward a second chance.'

We slept well that night. God's light had again shone down upon us, the freedom of innocents would continue.

Waking that morning, the children silently made their way downstairs, having dressed and readied for the day. They were spectacular. They made not a sound, ensuring their uncle, grandfather and mother slept peacefully in the morning.

I woke with them, making my way toward the kitchen. I felt lost. How Isabelle did it all, I would never know. I opted for a few eggs on toast. I believed it simple enough. Though scrambling the eggs was easier, I realised just how useless I was without her.

Burnt toast and dry eggs caused the children's great laughter, but they made their way towards the garden. A full day of playing was ahead of them. 'Twas a far cry from the courtyard where they once played.

A large woodland to the back of the house had them lost for the day. I took a paper and some tea on the back porch where I sat. The words of the paper blurred.

The odd few sounds of laughter shattered the silence of the morning. I thought of the countless lives we had saved.

In all, I spent the morning, trying to remember every one of them, by the end of the morning, two-hundred and thirteen had been saved by the family of God, and more were now waiting for us in the wings of the prison.

Riots had threatened our town before, starvation, robbery, theft. They all reached into the dark crevices of our town, but we would always be there to free those who deserved God's mercy.

Chapter Ten Judgement

allows Hill remained cold and empty. Isabelle convinced the judge who had convinced the council. The gaol would once again become the place where the condemned would die before being taken to the Marshes under the cover of darkness.

The chapel upon the site was fitted with new heavy wooden doors and locked. The grounds keeper had the chance to employ a night watchman. The town was content, knowing their lost loved ones were finally safe.

The following Friday, I was surprised to learn that Francis had insisted Isabelle allow the children to stay up late, giving him a chance to meet them.

Of course, upon our return to the house that night, my stomach was again churning, not knowing what Geoffrey had planned for the judge. It had been almost two years since I had hanged Timothy. I could still feel the bitterness from Geoffrey.

The house was warm stepping in, a fresh spring air came toward us from the back of the porch. The doors to the garden remained open, allowing a view of the gardens and the children playing in the woodland outside.

The evenings grew lighter. Summer would be harsh that year, but we were hoping for a plentiful year. Another winter of such meagre grain would see us to another riot.

They set the dining table. Bethany insisted upon sitting beside Francis.

Her eyes did not leave his face as we waited for Joseph and Isabelle to bring the evening meal.

'Bethany, please, stop staring,' I warned her, her tiny brown eyes continued glaring towards him. 'Bethany,' I scalded, her eyes broke, striking mine.

'But daddy, he's good to look at.'

'I apologise, Francis, children are strange creatures.'

'Worry not, I have seen plenty in my time.'

'You have a kind face, Sir, the face like a grandad.'

Her words warmed him. I had only seen Francis around the children of the gaol, and even then, the haunting dark wood of the docks separated them.

He reached towards her, placing an arm around her shoulder, he pulled her towards him for an embrace. Now I had seen everything, not only had my wife thawed his heart, but my children now caught the grandfather in him.

The evening went on, Geoffrey behaved. I could tell a simple scalding from his mother was enough to keep his tongue. He spoke nothing of Timothy, he spoke nothing of hanging, and nothing of the gaol.

The children retired, leaving us to more adult conversation. His talk of the town made me realise he had changed little.

'Poverty should be drowned like rats, for hundreds of years the church has made every attempt to rid these lands of the poor, constantly giving them all they need, and yet they still exist, it tells me, while there is a handout, there will always be the needy.'

'What of the more unfortunate?' Isabelle soon had to have her say. 'Mrs. Ackles, for example, born of a wealthy family, a hard-working husband and two children, life took a turn for her, during the riot she was trampled, now her husband is ill he can no longer work, and she is bed bound, does she not deserve the help of others?'

Francis shook his head. 'There will always be exceptions, Issy, but I speak of those who have no work but continue to reproduce.'

'I struggle to understand how people do not have a right to family.' Her argument was valid to me, but to Francis it was twisted.

'Would you have another child if your other children were in a poorhouse, would you consider more children, if you could not feed the ones you had? 'Tis selfish, and wrong, and we should not be expected to pay for those who cannot pay for their own way in life.'

'We pay our dues, Issy,' I quickly interjected, knowing she was losing her argument. She was too kind for the world of Francis.

'As we all should, leaving additional funds for those like Mrs. Ackles, so they have the funding when it is deserved and needed.'

Isabelle sat back, holding her back as she did.

'Won't be long now, Issy,' Joseph mentioned, looking at her wide belly. Joseph remained quiet of late; he ran his finger around the rim of his glass.

'If the child takes after its father, may God have mercy,' chuckled Francis.

'Twas no lie I was a large man, tall and broad at the shoulder. 'Well, the boy was a small birth, as was Bethany, but this one, I must say, Issy, even I'm concerned.'

'At least you'll have no business being there with this one, although, I would honestly prefer you were,' said Isabelle with a chastened look.

Francis looked at us both, confusion hit his aging face.

'You didn't know,' mumbled Joseph, a smug grin on his face was one I wished to wipe clear of him. 'Twas unheard of for a husband to be with his wife at such a time as labour. 'George here delivered both his children, was rather a heroic mission to say the least, from what I heard anyway.'

'George?' Francis's cold eyes drifted towards me.

'It was in no way heroic, in fact, the only one worthy of such a title was Issy, we were alone at the time, new to the town, she dropped just short of a two-day stay before we found a home, when Bethany was born, she was awkward, we'd spent the day in the grounds of the hall, upon arriving home, a mess was made.' I kept my eyes looking into hers. I would miss the arrival of our next child, but her insistence was we remained in the books of higher society.

'Why did you not call to someone?'

I laughed at his suggestion, 'This is the town of Nottingham, Francis, the first call of a labouring woman and the house becomes a target, at least it did in Peck Lane.'

'Well, at least now a good woman of repute will be by your side I trust.' I could see the worry he held, he genuinely cared for Isabelle. I was believing my thoughts of the judge were wrong.

'Of course, Mrs Morledge and her daughter, Clara, they will see me through the birth. If I have any worries or concerns, they have a physician on hand.'

I felt his relief as he relaxed back in his chair. I could see his eyes sagging. Tiredness had again set to us all.

The morrow brought a farewell to Francis. We made our way with him, seeing him at his gate, whereupon we ventured towards one of the friendlier pubs in the town.

Settled at the Bell Inn, Roderick, Joseph, and I chose a quiet corner. The stench of pipe smoke drowned the smell of stale ale out, the pub was small, but the brewing of ale at the pub provided a refreshing drink.

Making my way to the bar, I saw the landlord, William, clearing tankards from the bar.

'You're missing a trick, William. You should brew and sell. A few pubs in Mansfield would kick a horse for a keg as good as this.'

'You're too kind, George, although, we have been thinking of expanding of late, perhaps an investment, I see good land close to the Trent, would make for a great ground.'

'I'd be willing to invest. I could probably get a few on board.' I was impressed with William. They had seen not a single brawl in gone a month outside the Bell.

'Gentlemen!' called a watchman. He ambled his way into the establishment. He was all belt and braces, trying to intimidate. Usually, I would see him at the gaol, but the extra work had seen him to the streets that evening.

'Percy,' I grumbled with a wide grin. Stepping towards him, I looked down. His nerves shuddered at my presence.

'Evening, George,' his voice lowered, cowering like a cornered dog. 'I was simply here to speak with some of these gentlemen about the thefts from the Marshes.'

A man stood behind Percy caught my eye. I had seen him before within the town, a man who would always dress to impress the people of the town, but his skin would often turn people away.

Skin colour interested me. I could see the end of slavery within our fine town, and 'twas men like he who would end it.

Percy passed by, a slow step by step along the silent tables. The folks of the pub sat silently supping their ale.

'Evening.' I walked towards the tall black man, his wide and warm smile greeted me.

'You're George, is that correct?'

His deep voice was thrilling. 'That is Sir, and you are?'

'George also,' he carried an accent. He was well travelled, but a tinge of the exotic to his voice pulled me in further. 'George Africanus.'

'I must say, I admire men of the watch, especially those who are changing the faces of this town. I do not mean to be rude, I'm simply saying, men of colour, they are always welcomed by me.'

George gave a small snigger. I did not mean to offend him, I was simply trying to show gratitude to a race of people who were so cruelly persecuted.

'Issy was right.' I was surprised to hear him say the name of my wife, and he could clearly tell. 'I know her well, she often helps Ester, my wife, with small errands, we're not far from you, on Chandlers Lane, but of course now you've moved, I can only hope Issy will still make her journey to see Ester.'

'I knew nothing of this,' I chalked; however, Isabelle is a friend of all.

'It's true, but she often says you're a terribly busy man, and I see why. How is the child?'

'Well, she's yet to pop,' I mocked, 'when she does, I will be sure to bring her by.'

'I look forward to it, and of course Ester will, she has an affection for children, especially yours.'

'So, what brings you out here?'

He looked at Percy, posturing through the bar. 'I often get called up for the watch. It betters my standing in the town, and of course a man of colour. We need all the standing we can get.' He was mocking, but it was the truth. 'By day I'm a brass founder. Ester does all she can as a milliner from home.'

'A hard-working family, and it also explains Issy's growing collection of hats.'

Percy stormed towards us after speaking to a few at the bar.

'Come, this place is filled with the scum of the town. They won't talk,' he spat.

George widened his eyes, lifting his brows towards me.

'Perhaps, Percy, we could place you atop the chapel on the grounds. 'Tis but a foot wide, but a man as small as you would fit. You could be the new weathervane.' I wanted to make him feel as small as he made those in the pub feel.

'Come, George, a single gust would see him to his grave,' mocked William, the laughter of the pub resumed.

I know Percy heard us calling to him. George and his fellow Watchmen followed behind. They all towered over Percy, but his tiny stature was made up for with a terrible disposition.

Isabelle never failed to amaze me. Her way with people of the town saw all as a friend. Given that her husband was the executioner, some of those friends were none but fiends, praying upon the innocent sweetness of her.

Upon leaving the pub, a mist descended upon the town. A thick fog engulfed the centre of town, covering the building works and goings on.

A slow walk back saw us at our door. Roderick was the first to head inside. Joseph followed as I placed the carriage at the back of the lane. A strange air was with me that night. Seeing Percy in the pub was not strange, but his determination to find something as simple as a body snatcher had me baffled.

The persistence did not end. I joined Francis in his chambers that morning. A fresh batch of villains awaited us.

'Percy was busy last night, I see,' I mentioned, helping Francis on with his robes.

'He mentioned he saw you at the Bell on Angel row.' He turned to face me. 'Is this true?'

'It is, although I would rather not frequent such places, I like to keep my head within the crowd.' I saved myself from a scalding. He hated the thought of his men of the Lion frequenting anywhere else. 'He seems rather persistent, in finding those responsible for Marshes.'

'He is, a friend of his, 'twas a sad story, but I simply had no choice.' He was downcast. 'He was convicted of theft, last month, I believe his name was John, claimed he stole to feed his family, no excuse, when the coffins were inspected, his body was amiss, and Percy has been on the rampage since, John was Catholic, and they find grave disturbances worse than the Quakers.'

'So, a disturbance of a grave would see them to their pitches, I suppose.'

'Exactly that, and Percy is causing some disturbance already. I feel these walls rumbling. It should, however, keep people from crime, at least for a little while, knowing they will defile their bodies after death.'

"Tis true the thefts have seen a diversion of crime. Perhaps we should leave them to their work. They aren't harming anyone. You said it yourself. It simply aides in the discovery of science.'

'I am aware of this, George, but we must stop Percy before he causes damage.'

'Agreed, perhaps a stern word would see him to rights, I'll find him in the gaol later, see if I can knock some sense into the poor man.'

'I appreciate you, George, always there to ease a burden.'

I laughed, 'Percy is no burden, a small thorn in one's side is all. I shall have him calm by lunch.'

Leaving the judge to his duties, I set about finding Percy. He would frequent the part of the gaol saved for the adult offenders, a section we used to house those ready for the asylum. He enjoyed the bitter madness in the air.

'Percy,' I called, catching him swaying down one of the dark corridors, rattling his baton along the bars. 'A word, Percy?'

'A word of what?' his snarling already had me riled.

I caught him by the collar of his shirt, pulling him close. I whispered quietly, 'A word that will see you remain in these walls, and not within the bars.'

I took him to the gaoler's quarters. I could see my gallows through the window behind him. He sat with some hot tea I made fresh for him.

'What is this about?' His sighs riled me further, but I refused to show it.

Sitting at the front of him, I held a sympathetic tone.

'I know of your friend.' My admittance caused a crease at his brow. 'I know his remains were taken, I cannot know who by, Percy, but the man is dead, none escape the rope, his body is not your concern now, 'tis a death sentence you cast yourself to, if you do not refrain from such behaviour.'

'I know what he did was wrong, I will not argue with the law, George, and I will not argue with your ropes, but what they did to him, what they are doing to him, I know his family, they look to me for answers.'

Sitting back, I could see his quandary. I desperately wanted to tell him, but I knew our plan would unfold.

'Percy, Francis has noticed your disruptive actions.' He scowled towards me; he knew we were close friends. 'I simply wish to make your time at the gaol pleasing, to see you rise in the ranks, you are a good watchman, one of the best, I see you well within the rank of Constable, but your behaviour sees you in poor standing.'

His eyes softened. 'I will find him, George. Come next week, he will be at your gallows.'

'It is not a crime punishable by death.'

'You could sway the judge. Besides, I'm increasing the reward, from my pocket, to fifty guineas.'

'That is more than a wage to see a man at the end of days.'

'I know. The sale of my parents' house and a few bits collected from his family saw me fit. We will get him, George, if it is the last thing I do.'

My return home met with a dull mist. The house was quiet, the children were sitting in the parlour room reading. Isabelle sat in the kitchen, awaiting my return.

'Is everything alright?' Her bright voice was an instant warmth to me.

'I'm fine, just a small setback at the gaol.' Joseph made his way in from the back garden, carrying several potatoes Isabelle had planted.

'Set back?'

'Percy.' I looked at Joseph. 'The pustulous arsehole from the Bell, he's on a rampage to find the body snatchers, he's even gone so far to offer fifty guineas to the man who secures a conviction.'

'Fifty?' spouted Joseph, almost dropping the spuds. 'That's enough to see a man through to judgement.'

'Indeed, it is, which is why we must now be extra careful. Vigilance is needed if we are to continue God's work.'

I could feel their concern. We needed to carry on our work, until our day of judgement came. They could never catch us. God's children needed us.

Chapter Eleven The Shadow of Death

The streets echoed that day, a swirling sound of the bells from the church haunted me. Something was afoot. A crowd gathered. In the garden of Mr and Mrs Thackery-Jenkinson, a strange mood hit the street.

I approached the calling crowd, trying my best to pass by with some struggle. I could hear them calling to the crowd, another overly ambitious call for the Luddites to take their argument to parliament.

The town was changing; we had brought some change by showing mercy to the innocently guilty. Our business within God's family needed to change, as well. What we did was for a noble cause. I could feel the rope tightening. Noble cause or not, I knew we could not go on any longer without being caught.

The gaol was quiet. Hardly any passed through that day. Vagabonds and thieves, highwaymen, and robbers all lined the pitiful inside of the gaol.

The vagabonds of the town were mostly passing for the trade on the farms come harvest, but the harvest was far away. They chose the streets of Nottingham rather than Lincoln; we offered more for the poor. The churches would often open their doors to those waiting for the harvest.

The town was running peacefully as spring appeared. With only a few weeks left for our new infant to arrive, I would not be as busy as the winter had seen. Francis appeared to be in an effervescent mood, constantly being fed by Isabelle and her addictive smile and joy.

A few hangings were scheduled for that week, a better mood with Francis saw only the deserving upon the dock, until he came, a man of good reputation stood upon the dock, I knew his name as John Corn, a farmer who once lived in Derby, had joined the industry being developed in Nottingham.

'My name is John Corn, Sir.'

'The crime in which I charge you with, is one heinous act of arson, please, explain yourself.'

'I hardly know where to begin, Sir, I was nowhere near the home when it became a blaze.'

The only fire I knew of was the home of Rose and her mother. I had heard of nothing since.

I listened to the plea from John Corn. 'I knew Rose and Gladys, lovely girls, I would never bring harm to them.'

The prosecution stood, and this was where his rope tightened. 'You argued with them.'

"Twas but a misunderstanding,' he proclaimed. He clearly felt ill at the thought of angering the women. 'They believed me to be from a man who was trying to buy their farm. They say he used aggressive tactics.'

'Did you not think it strange they had not reported it to the authorities?'

'I believed they had. I was simply interested in the land at the back of the farm, not the place itself. I saw an opportunity, but it certainly was not worth killing over.'

'Did you know they were home that night?'

'Well, no.'

'So, you admit you were there?'

'No, I said before, I was not there.'

'Then how do you know they were not home?'

'I did not know if they were home or not. I do not know. I wasn't there.'

'Then explain the account from a Mrs. Mayberry, I quote, your honour, 'I hereby witnessed Mr. Corn skulking about the property of Rose and Gladys Stoppard, whereupon I noted a large rod in his hand, I passed by walking down the lane towards Leen Side, 'twas shortly after, as the hour led towards the early hour of 3 in the morn, I noticed a bellowing smoke from the farm, whereupon I alerted my neighbours, and we found the authorities to extinguish the flames.'

I saw him squirming on the dock, ringing his cap in his hands, a sweat began to settle upon his forehead. He still wore a large brown overcoat, the sort that was slowly coming into fashion.

'I was simply curious,' he stuttered. 'I was not there to harm them. I simply showed concern for them. Rose worried about the men who were bothering them.'

'Did you see anyone there that night?'

'I wasn't there, not when the fire began. I was there upon the evening, at dusk, but I left shortly thereafter. I saw no one else there.'

'So, you have lied to this court, about being there that night, you were there, Mr. Corn, and I put it to you, during your time there,' — the voice of the prosecution rose as he delivered the man's death sentence. — 'You saw no one, in a moment of maddened rage you saw your chance, getting the property would see your new mill upon the Leen, you would find riches from your investment, but those women stood in your way, so you took your stick, you lit the flame and watched them burn, under the cover of darkness you fled, awaiting the land to be a place for sale.'

'Francis, are you hearing this?' John asked, turning to Francis. I was shocked he knew the man, but clearly, they were well acquainted.

'I hear it all, John, and I must say, you lied about being there at all, who is to say, you are not lying about it all, an honest man must remain so, or see his lies unfold upon the dock.'

I knew Francis now; I knew the look he held, a troubled look of remorse, he was not the callous judge I thought him to be; he was controlled, those controlling him held power in the town, a power he longed to know, but he was but a humble judge, sending his own friends to my gallows.

The entire trial was only a few minutes. He read a verdict of guilty. He would see my rope, but if he would see mercy, was yet for me to figure out.

I made my way into the chambers of Francis as the day ended. He was pleased to see me.

'Not in the gaol today?'

'Not all day. I enjoy watching you work, Francis. However, that business with John Corn. How do you know him?'

I took his cloak, helping him on with it. 'It was a mistake many years ago, he was invited into the Lion, he embarrassed himself with talk of industry, claiming the waters surrounding Nottingham were not treated properly, he proposed, with a healthy investment of twenty guineas from each member, he would see a healthy solution to our water, and with that, we would see a healthy return.'

'Sounds promising. Why would he embarrass himself with such talk?'

'Because, asking members for an investment is one thing, he was practically insisting, taking advice from the sellers of snake oil, telling people they were drinking raw sewerage without his help, he was banned from the chambers for such vulgar talk, he went too far and I warned him, now he seems to have turned to murder to get his own way.'

'Francis, you know 'twas not John Corn, you know who it was, don't you?'

I walked by his side toward the gates of the gaol, placing his hat upon his head. He turned to face me.

'See him yourself if you please, George, but remember, the man has a poor reputation within our society. Our circle of friends would not be pleased if you befriend a man so, dauncy.'

'I would still wish to speak to him. The farm has been the subject of a few disputes now.'

'It would sit better with me if you didn't, George. The land is now sold, prying will only get you into trouble.'

'Then what is his crime, Francis, how can you so easily send a man to his death?'

He could sense my anger and concern.

'George, we tread thin ice daily. John Corn will get what he deserves.' He saw me draw back, softening his look towards me. 'He threatened to talk, to expose our innermost sins of the Lion's Chambers. We cannot allow it, George.'

'So, you take his life instead. Why do I feel you know more about this, Francis?'

'Because I do, my duty within the Lion keeps me in good standing in this town, as it does you, I do what I do to survive in a town ruled by the higher-class, you would do well to follow my example.' He straightened up, stood beside the heavy wooden door.

'Remember, George, we all have family, they are the ones we protect, regardless of our indiscretion, the Lions of the Chambers will always place their murders in the hands of the court, making them appear free of their sins, they kill, and we make it look lawful, it is the way of the Lions.'

It all made sense to me now, those who burnt the farm did not need to drag Rose through court, they could've destroyed the farm anyway, however, if the Lion's Chambers were to take all they wanted, murder would have increased in the town, making our city status impossible to find, they needed every death to look legitimate, turning them into criminals was their way of securing the future of their town.

'Enough of such unpleasant business. Will you join me this evening at the Lion?'

I gave a warm smile; I did not wish to raise his suspicion. 'I believe Roderick is already there, so I will be along later.'

'Good, now stay away from business where you do not belong, George.'

He made his way down the steps, walking towards his carriage, which would take him directly to the Lion's Chambers.

His words stuck with me, but I needed to know for myself.

When I saw him in his cell, he had not lost hope. John paced the floor. As he saw me approach, he clung to the bars; he had not shed a single tear; he worried a reprieve had not yet seen him.

'I'm going to make this a little different for you. First, you are to remain quiet.' I always had to be different with all, but he was the type who would not comply.

'Who are you?'

'My name is George, and I am your executioner.'

'I would say 'tis a pleasure, but given the unfairness of these circumstances, I cannot say such a thing. I was there that afternoon, but come the dusk I left, I would never cause harm to those women.'

'I know.' I kept my voice quiet, knowing the passing gaolers would often creep around corners. 'However, I need more convincing. What do you know about the men who set the farmhouse alight?'

'I know nothing, I was gone before they arrived, however, Rose told me it was a man called Durham, he was attempting to purchase the land for a wealthy lord, I tried to convince her to sell to him, they were dangerous, I saw them in the town, in the Lion.'

It struck me like a bolt, I knew the duties of the Lion went beyond the mistreatment of youth, and I knew the Lion was for elevating positions within the town, but now I had it confirmed, the deaths of many led back to the Lion, no one was safe within the town, not while the Lion stood.

'Is there anyone we can trust?' asked Roderick. Joseph walked silently behind us. His silence was unnerving.

The bells began their haunting deep toll. I replied, 'I have a few, but I can no longer trust those within the town.'

'Then you must ask their council, we can not take down the Lion, not alone, George, this is bigger than executions now, 'tis bigger than God's family, we can only do so much.'

'When will the next hangings be?' Joseph called out.

'You won't be needed until next week. We have only two scheduled so far.'

'And what of John Corn?' asked Joseph.

'I am yet to decide. He appears innocent, and I truly believe he is, but his insistence cannot place us in jeopardy, and I fear it will.'

'How so?' asked Roderick.

'Each one we save must leave Nottingham and never return. However, I feel his persistence will see him remain, which makes it dangerous.'

'Have you explained this to him, he can never return, he can never be John Corn again?' Roderick asked.

'Not yet, I'll see him again on the morrow.'

Stepping into the house, screams of anguish met us, Mrs Thatcher ran towards us, an old grey woman who had taken it upon herself to help Isabelle in her trouble.

'The child is on its way, please, to the kitchen with all of you. We have everything in hand.'

I could see Mrs Morledge pass by behind her. Her wide smile comforted me; Isabelle's huffing screams did not bring comfort.

'How's Issy,' my panic caught her. A husband in that area would rarely show concern for his wife.

'Your wife is well, she will be fine, now please, a hearty drink will see you through this night.'

Roderick and Joseph guided me towards the kitchen, where the sounds and calls became muffled by the thick walls.

A thought suddenly hit me. 'Joe, would you do me a great favour? Go to the home of Francis, tell him the news.'

Joseph stood, running towards the carriage at the front.

'He will be most pleased,' I said to Roderick. I felt my head grow light. 'I don't know how to do this, I was always there for her, and now I am expected to leave her to the hands of others, whom I barely know.' I looked at the door, I could feel myself picking at my fingers, a habit I only had when nerves hit me.

It felt like a lifetime we were waiting, waiting for that call, the sound of serenity, the sound of unconditional love. The sound of a baby's cry called out. Roderick lifted his head from low upon the table. His smile widened. He looked towards me. I shook with glee.

I stood, making my way towards the parlour. I would've heard that call from a thousand miles away. A slowness hit me as I entered the room, seeing Mrs. Thatcher carrying my new son towards me, they saw the tear in my eye; I let it freely drop, holding my son for the first time, I dropped at the side of Isabelle, her soft kiss reassured me, she would survive the closest thing to death.

The door opened; Mrs and Miss Morledge worked to make Isabelle presentable for our esteemed guest. Francis turned at the front door. Upon seeing me in the parlour, beside myself with joy, he walked towards me.

'I did not expect you to come,' I gasped, breathless at the beauty in the room.

'Poppycock, I would not miss such an occasion.' He held his arms out. 'Twas the human side of Francis I always enjoyed seeing, a side which had shown itself more in the company of God's family.

Isabelle was well, the child was a quiet one, sleeping peacefully through the night he woke only for a single feed from her.

Our family had grown, with the addition of Peter Francis Smith, a name chosen by Isabelle, which made Francis giddy at the announcement.

I awoke early on the morning of John Corn's execution. Isabelle readied the children. Stepping into the kitchen, she handed me one of the men's jackets, ready for my decision. John had made an excellent student, he had learnt. I only hoped he would stay away from Nottingham upon his eventual fate.

'I'll be waiting in the lane,' said Isabelle, handing me a loaf of lavender bread to deliver to Francis.

'No, you won't,' I warned. 'Joe will take care of everything, and Roderick, they can handle a single man. You remain here with the children.'

'I love to see them, though,' complained Geoffrey.

'I understand, but you have another duty now, one more important than the saving of men. You must both help your mother in the home, ensure all is ready for when I return.' I looked at Isabelle. 'I'm only going to assume Francis will wish to return with me tonight, so, I'll be home early, get some rest.'

Kissing her forehead, I bid my final farewell. The town was still sleeping as I left, ready to be woken by the sound of the tolling bells. The ground shook with their sounding.

Upon arriving at the gaol, I made my way towards the yard, passing Percy as I did.

'Morning.'

'It is,' he sighed. He had become more bitter, knowing his plan to catch the grave robbers had failed.

'Come on, Percy, I doubt they are even still here, probably moved on to Lincoln or Derby by now. Calm yourself.'

'I will. When I see John hang, I liked Rose, knowing what he did boils my piss.'

'Well then, follow me, Roderick left early to prepare the prisoner, grab a cup and wait in the gaoler's room, shouldn't be too long.'

My invite for Percy to take tea worked, giving me a chance to dress John in his jacket.

'You remember what we discussed?' His frantic nod showed the fear in his eyes.

'I can never return. I understand, George, I understand. I would never wish to return to such a cursed town.'

Leading him toward the gallows, I repeatedly had to warn him, to show an emotion. He tried to cry, but I believe 'twas a cry of elation he showed more than anything.

John Corn would at last be free from the town, his troubles, and his downward reputation.

He flailed like a leaf in the breeze, legs kicking became twitching, he died good and proper. Percy remained with bloodlust in his eyes upon the steps to the gaoler's chambers.

Placing John in his eternity box, we left the room, noticing Percy's persistence. He locked the door to the room, taking a small wooden chair at the side, he slumped down.

'What are you doing, Percy?' I asked derisively, although I did not mean to.

'Just a watch. I plan on following these two to their last resting place and taking a watch on the Marshes.'

I looked at Roderick. 'Well, give me a shout if you need anything, I'm sure I'll hear.' 'Twas all I could think to say, we would be taking John and William, the guilty, to Broad Marshes that afternoon, with Percy in tow, we needed to make it quick.

Joseph had made his way towards the lane with an empty coffin in tow, weighed with bricks.

Percy did indeed follow, but he was on foot, opting to take my advice. Walking would allow him to see any ne'er-do-wells hanging around near the burial grounds.

It would allow mere seconds for us to make the crucial switch. We stopped the carriage close to the lane, the thick walls covered us, changing the coffin from one to the other, placing it upon the carriage in the lane I heard an echoing voice call.

'Halt!' I felt my heart burst with fear. A strange fullness in my head had me panicked. Turning toward Bridle Smith Gate, the Watchmen came rushing towards us.

'Joe, go!' I called to him. He remained silent on the carriage. I knew, from that second, I knew he was not a man of God.

'Joe, why?'

'You would risk my sister, for the sake of guilty men, George. This needed to stop.' Those were the last words I heard from him. Percy rushed up the lane. Upon seeing Joseph, he paid him no heed.

'Men, arrest them, for aiding and abetting in the escape of convicts, for committing the most heinous of crimes, George Smith, and Roderick Dresden, I hereby inform you of your arrest.'

I watched Roderick struggle into his shackles. A hissing pain in his voice spat at Joseph. 'You are no son of mine, and you are not in the family of God.'

My heart sank. I fell to my knees, light in the head, unable to breathe properly. They separated me and Roderick.

I never thought I would see the other side of those bars. The cells were colder than I remembered; the air was thinner; the gaol was once my home, but now it was my worst enemy. I felt shame for what I had done, but I could not, for that would question the path God had set me. I would not question God.

They spared me no embarrassment. Before they brought my charges to me upon the dock, he came. From the corridor, I heard the shuffling footsteps.

Peering around the corner, the face of Francis peered towards me. I shot to my feet, but I had no words to say. A chastened look was all I could give.

'You betrayed me, George.' I knew I hurt him, but I hurt too. 'You betrayed my trust, you brought me into your family, and for what?'

'Because I know you are a good man.' I felt a burning behind my eyes, a painful remorse ready to break.

'I am a good man, George. I send murderers to their death, and here you were, saving them.'

He looked at me with such disgust. 'No, please, Francis, I saved none of them, only the ones who deserved a second chance, a chance to go with God—'

'God has no place within these walls. God will decide when they arrive at his gate. We are here to send them, but you—'

'Francis, please, I only chose those who would go with God, those who were stealing for food, the children, who wanted nothing more than a family, Francis, please, I would never save a murderer.'

He stepped back from the bars. Percy, the snivelling git, stepped to the side of him, holding the jacket up.

'Where is his body?' He was an idiot, he still did not understand.

'With his spirit still, Percy, he was innocent. He made his way with the others, to live a free life. He deserved a second chance.'

'He's still alive.' I saw his lip quiver. Elation and guilt hit him hard. 'You saved him?' A tear fell from his eye.

'Yes,' I whispered to him, knowing his good friend was innocent.

'Percy, make your way to the Lion. Wait for me there,' ordered Francis.

Percy was broken. I could feel it. His sunken face turned from me, knowing what he had done. He would carry to his grave with him, so many innocents would die because of his inability to heed my warning.

'What now?' I asked, desperate for a reprieve.

'You deceived me, George, I trusted you and I loved your family, the Lion is already speaking of your crime, this will see you to the gallows, George, as for Issy, I will do my best, but Joe told us everything.'

'Francis, what of the children?' I begged. He turned to leave me alone in my misery, forcing my screams, 'Francis! What of my children? What of my father?'

He turned, a callous look of anguish on his face growled towards me. 'They are no longer your children, George.'

The echoes of the gaol lasted the night. Knowing the hangman was in the cell beside them, it charged the air, making their howling of insanity even more prevalent.

The evening lingered, the ghosts in the darkness of the corridors leered towards me. I could feel the icy grasp of death upon me, rather than panic, or pray for salvation, I made peace with my fate.

An echoing in the corridor roused me. I could hear echoing voices. The closer they came, the closer I made my way toward the bars.

The faces of those men glared at me. Francis walked toward the bars, all of them in tow. The Lion's Chambers had clearly been alight with talk of my arrest.

'George.' Francis showed a nervous disposition. 'My esteemed colleagues are concerned—'

'George, your position in the Lion saw you privileged to certain information, a warning to you, George, that information is to die with you, or your family will be by your side in death.' Godfrey's words cut worse than a rope.

'You threaten my family?' I looked at Francis. I believed he would do nothing to harm them. He would never allow such a thing.

'George, it is out of my hands now, Durham is involved, the chambers are in uproar, a trial will need to be heard, so the people of this town do not see reason for another riot, Isabelle has explained everything, she knows the people, however, your trial must go ahead, with silence from you.'

'I have a request.' I had a thought, a slight idea, it would not secure my freedom, but it would prevent the suffering of countless others. 'Parchment and pen, that is all I request.'

Francis turned his dying eyes to the others. His guilt was clear. He did not wish to see me hang, and I needed him to know I did not blame him.

'Francis, this is no doing of yours, I apologise for the ills I have brought to your court, and I deeply apologise if you feel I have deceived you, but you were my friend, Francis, and the best uncle my children ever had, please, keep Joseph away from the children, you are their guardian now.'

I could see his frosty glare melt; he did not wish to
show such emotion in front of those men.

'Come, Francis, he has his warning.' I watched him
walk with Godfrey down the corridor. The men stopped
at the end, their echoing voices met me.

'What now? There are criminals roaming this country,
all from Nottingham, all with links back to here.'

'No, we destroy it all, every record, every name, we
bury them, it would make a mockery of this town, every
one of his hangings is to be wiped from our books, we
will wipe his family; his name will no longer plight these
walls.' The pain-filled voice of Francis hit me. They
would bury everything, cover everything. They would be
sure to hide it all, for the sake of their own skins, and for
the sake of the town of Nottingham.

The night lingered, several of the gaolers passed my
bars, all refused to look me in the eye, I did not know if
it was because of their lack of sympathy, or their
heightened sympathy, either way, I would've done
anything for a conversation.

'George,' I heard a whisper, a voice I knew. Standing at
the cold bars, I saw a shadow approach.

'Percy?' squinting my eyes, I could just about see him.
'Why are you here?'

'I offered a shift. I needed to speak to you.' The guilt
he felt quivered in his voice. 'I didn't know what you

were doing. I believed— I don't know what to believe anymore.'

He turned his back, resting against the bars. "Tis no fault of yours, Percy. I did what I did, because those men, women and children, they were innocent.'

'Children.' He shook his head, looking down. 'How has it come to this, George, where a child is no longer free to be as God intended?'

I saw he was a man of God, a man of truth and justice, a man like me. 'Percy, I have a request of you, you can tell me no, but it would help our town greatly, and it would aide in the recovery of Nottingham.'

He turned toward the bars. 'Anything.'

'I need you to get a letter to the priest of Clifton church for me, St Mary's. Can you do that?'

'Of course I can. I was born there, so I know him well.'

'Return here in two days. I shall have the letter for you.'

The days slowly passed; I was yet to see the trial.

The stench of the gaol changed. I was used to a freshness in the air, a freshness which eluded me in the cells. A stagnant stench of fear, old broth gave a smell of rotten milk.

Gregory paced towards my cell; he carried a large tray.

'Here, George, the wife sent some stew. She wouldn't see you have any of the filth we have here, oh, and this.' He passed a parchment and pen through the bars towards me.

'I appreciate that, Greg, and I appreciate you, 'tas been a pleasure working with you.'

'Don't, George, I cannot see your crime, and having you behind those bars, it makes us all see, just how vulnerable we are. In fact, there is an additional problem in the gaol, they're refusing to hang you, not a single gaoler will set forth to pull that lever.'

'I will gladly pull it myself, knowing the truth is out in our town.'

'We will listen to everything you say, George, but the safety of our families is already at risk. We are lost, George.'

I clung to the bars, looking into his eyes. 'Greg, I will be with God.' I held a smile, hiding my fear. 'I cannot deny my family is the only thing I will miss, but I know that my men at the gaol will care for them, my fate is sealed, and now, I will seal the fate of Nottingham.'

'Do what you must, George.' He could see my desperation. The gaol took the soul before the body, and it had with me.

'Isabelle is well, they have warned her away from the gaol, they've refused her entry. I saw the children this morning, walking along Stoney Street towards lessons.

The bane is growing well.' His deep sigh spoke of the awkwardness he felt. He could barely look at me.

'Greg, I hope you will see them each morn.' I allowed my tears to fall. 'Remind them of me, please.'

'I will.'

I spent the entire two days, sleepless, frantically writing all I could. I told of the Lion's Chambers, the atrocities there, the countless lives that had been saved, from unfair punishments, lacking evidence, those who died, because their property was wanted by others, I told more than I knew to be the truth, I wrote my confession, Percy collected my notice. I was forced to trust.

I had not seen Isabelle for our last farewell. Now I knew how the others felt. No chance to see their loved ones before they passed.

They gave me no graces at trial. Francis remained silent on his bench. He asked no questions; the prosecution asked nothing, even the jury remained silent.

'Twas an odd trial. They all refused to speak first, leaving the first comment to me.

'My name is George Smith, I am guilty, of the crime of which I am charged.' I looked at Francis, I did not know if I would see him again. 'Francis, let this be my final plea to you.' He looked at me. I could see his jaw swell to the side, clenching his teeth, holding tears, as his lips curled and shook.

'Francis, you have become my dearest friend, in the gaol, and out, I urge you, retire.' I pleaded with him, knowing I could say little, fearing they would discover my final plea. A letter to be sent to the chief justice, telling of their crimes, annulling Francis of any wrongdoings in the house of justice.

'Become the head of the family of God and see yourself free of your sins of the Lion.' I saw them glaring towards me, the faces from the Lion's Chambers. They paid no attention to the words I spoke, 'twas the ramblings of a condemned man.

They forced me from the court, sent to rot in my cell for the last few days. A punishment was not even called. Like all the others before mine, the trial was nothing but a show.

The pub was empty. The smell of stale ale invited me in for my last pint of Nottingham Ale. I held my head bloody high, the landlord stared at me, we even toasted.

'Going to miss you around here, George,' he said, polishing a few tankards and placing them back behind the bar.

'You know what, I'll miss the people here too, Tommy, but the rest of it, can burn in hell.' I didn't know my words, I prayed at the bar; I prayed for a reprieve, but nothing came.

'Come, George,' called Connor. They had requested the hangman from Lincoln to assist in my hanging. My old assist John had grown well. He had learnt a lot from Connor, and from me.

The familiar faces were gone from Gallows Hill. They had opened the gallows just for me. I would have been flattered, but knowing I would be put straight to the ground at the Marshes was no comfort to me.

Connor Ashworth had a way with hanging, covering his face I found to be a cowardly act. I would soon learn why Francis insisted on a comfortable rope, 'twas the last comfort I knew in this life.

'Remove his shirt.' The remorse in the gaoler's voice was clear. The executioner reluctantly opened my shirt. My hands remained tied at the back of me. They were checking, making sure I did not have a jacket of life.

I was not ready to go with God. I wanted only the comfort of my family. I felt my tears freely flow down my face, muttering the lord's prayer. I could only hope I had made him proud.

The rope tightened, the pain was worse than I thought, my body fought, I tried to go as quickly as I could. Every face I had saved, every life I had ended, they were all there. They all whispered the same words, the words I would always say within their ultimate moments. 'Go with God, George,' I heard their faint whisper. And then the darkness came.

A flickering glow lit the street outside. In her misery, Isabelle sat, alone. The children laid in their beds. Dull embers from the fire reflected an orange hue from her wet, tear-filled face.

A knock at the door startled her. Slowly, she stood. The house had been busy that day, George's crimes had spread through the town like fire, but the people, the real people of Nottingham, knew he died an innocent man, bent on saving them.

Upon opening the door, Percy stood with a letter in his hand. He awkwardly hurried to remove his hat and hold it at the front of him. His beady eyes drifted down, sweat wet his hair.

'Ma'am, I apologise for being a disturbance at such a time as this, but I need a talk.'

Isabelle opened the door, her mouth remained agape.

'I know you; I saw you often at the gaol. Are you Henry's nephew?' she asked.

Percy quickly nodded; quick movements of his body showed his shot nerves.

'You are also the man responsible for this.' Her voice was soft, exhausted from anger, tears, and grief.

'I am,' he whispered with his head low.

'I,' — Isabelle struggled to speak, — 'I don't blame you, and you cannot blame yourself, you didn't know.' Tears tumbled from her eyes, dripping on the top ruffle of her dress.

'I should have,' whispered Percy. 'He tried to tell me, but I didn't listen, I couldn't listen.'

Isabelle reached out, placing her hand on his shoulder.

'I came here, to give you something.' He held the letter up. 'Before he... before they took him, George wrote a letter, said to take it to the church at Clifton.'

'Then why didn't you?' asked Isabelle.

'Because the bastards at the Lions have said that if anything gets out, they'll come after you and the kids. I will do all I can, miss, so will the lads at the gaol, but those men are evil, we won't be able to stop them.'

Isabelle sauntered towards the living room, stumbling as she did. She took a seat on the sofa, reading the letter, it recounted their crimes.

'I have lost my husband, my father is sent to foreign lands, and my brother found guilty of the murder of a whore's guardians and set to die tomorrow.' Her misted eyes looked at Percy. 'How can I take anymore?'

He rushed towards her. 'No matter what you choose to do, we swore to George we would look after you.'

She shook her head as she looked down. 'I can't do this anymore.'

'Miss, you saved so many innocent lives. Perhaps, now it's time for you to rest, don't run, let someone else bear the weight for a while. Raise your babies.'

Isabelle stood, throwing the letter into the last embers of the fire, which clung to the pages.

'We didn't fail,' she whispered. 'You can leave now, Percy. Thank you, for being his friend, in the end.'

A Brief History of Nottingham

Nottingham Gaol

Now an award-winning visitor centre, the Nottingham gaol plays host to the ghosts of the past. The Nottingham County Gaol dates to at least 1375, the prison dates to at least 1449 and closed in 1878.

It would have seen lawbreakers from all over the county of Nottinghamshire, from thieves to highwaymen. Many of the crimes punishable by death, would today, be deemed as frivolous and a waste of court resources.

The gaol was well known for its poor living conditions, its meagre rationing of food and torturous way of treating human beings.

Things were to change within the prison systems, which began with John Howard, Esq. On behalf of the Duke of Montagu, he was employed to carry out a review of the midlands prison systems.

Howard's aim was to review the living conditions of the prisons, and the prisoners themselves. His review brought to light the poor conditions prisoners had to suffer.

Howard reported,

'The Morals of prisoners were at this time as much neglected as their health. Idleness, drunkenness and all kinds of vice, were suffered to continue in such manner as to confirm old offenders in their bad practices, and to render it almost certain, that the minds of those who were confined for their first faults, would be corrupted, instead of being corrected, by their imprisonment.'

Howard went on to criticise the prison systems, making some recommendations that remain to this day.

'Every prison be white washed at least once a year, and that is to be done twice in prisons which are much crowded.

That a pump and plentiful supply of water be provided, and that every part of the prison is to be kept as clean as possible.

That every prison be supplied with a warm and cold bath, or commodious bathing tubs, and that the prisoners be indulged in the use of such baths, with proper allowance of soap and the use of towels.

That attention be paid to the sewers in order to render them as little offensive as possible.

That great care be taken, that as perfect a separation as possible be made of the following classes of prisoners.

That felons be kept entirely separate from the debtors; men from women, old offenders from young beginners; convicts from those who have not yet been tried.

That all prisoners, except debtors, be clothed on their admission with a prison uniform and their own clothes be returned to them when they are brought to trial or are dismissed.

That care be taken that the prisoners are properly supplied with food, and their allowance not deficient, either in weight or quality.'

He also recommended that the gaolers were to be paid a proper wage, religious services were to be added, swearing was to be banned. Upon their discharge from the prison, Howard also insisted provisions be put into place, to help prisoners if they may be unable to make an honest wage.

Policing in Nottingham Town

The Nottinghamshire Constabulary was established in 1840. Before this time, the first constable was Richard  Birth from 1814 to 1833. The town would have seen many voluntary watchmen, as well as many employed by the county sheriff. The streets would have been governed by watchmen and police, keeping the county safe from criminal activity was a growing concern within parliament, which caused many acts to be passed, policing was on the increase, and so was crime.

History of Hanging

The Nottingham Gaol was not as infamous as people thought for hanging, with very few hangings a year, those within the above book would have been:

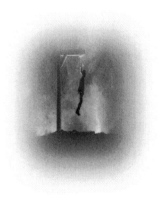

1799. James Brodie, for murder.

1800. John Atkinson, for forgery.

1801. Michael Denman, William Sykes and Thomas Bakewell, for forgery.

1802. Mary Voce, for murder.

1802. Ferdomamdp Davis, for highway robbery.

1803. John Thompson, for robbery.

1803. William Hill was hung August 10, for committing a rape (attended with great brutality), on the person of Mrs Sarah Justice, the wife of a respectable farmer, near Gainsborough, on the 28th of the previous May. He acknowledged to the Chaplin, after conviction, that he had made criminal attempts upon other females, one of whom was only 12 years of age, but without success. The Chaplin, and a number of pious persons, attempted to soften the ferocity of his disposition, by representing to him the extent of his crime, and the danger of dying in hardened state, but all their efforts proved to be in vain. On the morning of death, he manifested the most extreme reluctance to submit to the sentence of the law. He had to be dragged out of his cell by force, and the exertions of half-a-dozen men were scarcely sufficient for the task of pinning him. He was then conveyed in the customary manner to Gallows-hill; but no sooner did he feel the cord loose by which he was tied to the cart, that he leapt over the side of the vehicle, and endeavoured to escape, to the great astonishment and agitation of the multitude. Several of the Sheriff's men immediately struck him with the blunt end of javelins, and in spite of his horrid language and struggles, he was again forced to ascend the cart, and compelled to meet his fate.

1805. Robert Powell, alias Harvey, for robbery.

1806. William Rhodes, alias Davies, for forgery.

1809. Thomas Lampin, for forgery.

1812. Benjamin Renshaw, for firing a haystack.

The last public execution was that of Richard Thomas Parker, in **1864**, for murder.

The last execution to take place in Nottingham was that of George Hayward, in **1928**, for the murder of Amy Collinson.

Gallows Hill

Gallows Hill remains infamous to this day, situated at the top of Mansfield Road, the gallows would have warned any traveling into the town from the north, that they would punish their crimes in the most brutal way possible.

Those hanged at Gallows Hill would have found their final resting place at the Broad Marshes Burial Ground until the new Church (Rock) Cemetery was built in 1851. The Broad Marshes Burial Ground, which was part of what now stands as St Peters Church, was exhumed in 1960. The graves were moved to the Wilford Hill Cemetery.

The Church (Rock) Cemetery now serves many of the parishes in Nottingham. It holds some key history to the town of Nottingham. Many urge it as a 'must' to visit when in the city.

Pubs and places of note.

The Nags Head, Mansfield Road is now a sad story, like many of Nottingham's buildings, the pub became redundant and empty, plans were put in place to turn it into student accommodation in 2019, although this caused arguments from both locals and historical societies. Plans could not be carried out because of the global pandemic. At the time of publication, the pub still stands empty.

Nottingham is steeped in history, dating back to the doom's day books of 1066, the church of St Marys in Clifton, as well as several other pubs such as The Bell, Ye Olde Trip to Jerusalem and The Salutation Inn, bring the history of the town to life.

Many of the different buildings surrounding Nottingham can make for a fun family day out, but the history surrounding such places also pays tribute to our ancestors who built the town.

Quakers

The history of the quakers dates to the 17th century. They have worshiped in Nottingham since 1648, with their first meeting house being a private house on Spaniel Row, which was purchased in 1678.

In 1649, George Fox arrived in Nottingham. He interrupted the service at St Mary's Church and was subsequently imprisoned for this. The wife of the Sheriff, who attended the church that day, was so influenced by George Fox, she arranged his removal from the prison, which was then at the Weekday Cross, he was released into the custody of the sheriff, he and his wife soon afterwards became quakers.

George Africanus

Nottingham has long been associated with the black community, one man of note is George Africanus, born in Sierra Leone, he came to live with his family at Molyneux House, Wolverhampton, where he rose to the position of manservant and was taught to read, write, and subtract. The family paid for George to learn the trade of Brass founder. Slavery was coming to an end, and in 1784, he completed his service with the family, and came to live in Nottingham.

He married Ester Shaw at the St Peter's Church. They had six children. Only one, however, survived to adulthood.

In 1820, he was the keeper of the 'Registrar Office of Servants,' an employment agency which placed servants with the high-class families in Nottingham. As a property owner, he was also able to vote in parliamentary elections, he was also a member of the watch and ward register.

George Africanus died aged 71, on May 24th 1834, and was buried at St Mary's Churchyard.

Waterways and the Leen

It was notable that the River Leen supplied Nottingham with most of its water throughout the 1800s. This was until it was noticed that the waterway was contaminated with raw sewerage.

The Nottingham Waterworks Company was the first recorded public waterworks company in 1696. The new Nottingham Waterworks company took over in 1845 until 1974, when the Severn Trent Water Authority was created.

Luddites

From 1811 to 1816 the Nottingham Luddites began riots. They destroyed machinery, especially in cotton and woollen mills, that they believed were threatening their jobs. The Luddite's movements ended with the harsh sentence being passed. Parliament made 'machine 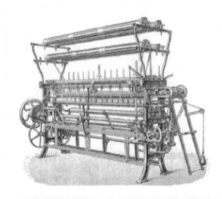 breaking' a capital crime, with the frame-breaking act of 1812. Many of the Luddites were sentenced to death during this time across the country.

Nottingham Lace

The invention of the knitting frame by William Lee of Calverton in Nottinghamshire changed the area and eventually gave the Lace Market its name.

Richard Arkwright established a small cotton mill in Hockley, in 1768. Lace was manufactured on a frame adapted from that of William Lee and was further improved by John Heathcote and John Levers in the early 19th century. By the 1840s, lace making was changing from a domestic industry into an international export.

Nottingham a final note

Nottingham grew so vastly it was given a city status in 1897. It remains steeped in hidden history and has been noted as an area of historical significance. Nottingham remains a place of diversity and acceptance. The different areas of Nottingham County bring it together as a city of explorers, a place of deep history and a place of valued history.

While I built the above story of George Smith of fiction, conspiracy theories have long been prevalent among the higher classes ruling certain areas of the town and county.

During the writing of this, I have found myself in a hard position. In 2019, a global pandemic placed the world on hold. While we mourned for those we had lost, it also opened us to a new world.

The city of Nottingham has a reputation now of being a place of violent outbursts, crime, drugs, and worse. As a novelist, I would usually spend my time within the city archives, trying to discover the town that way. However, with the lockdown of Nottingham, the streets have become my archives.

A final note on Nottingham, and my advice to many, whether you live in Nottingham, or you are simply visiting, I urge all to look up. When visiting the city centre, look at the buildings, the rich, deep history, which can be seen from the market square, where the old gas lanterns light the streets, all the way through the city, from the towering buildings of industry to the small streets and alleyways which once held housing for those within the town.

The ghosts of the past follow all through the town centre. It has long been a place of corruption and compassion, a place of acceptance and inequality.

The Market Square itself, once known as the Great Market Place, dates to the 11th century, although many changes have been made since, some building still stand, such as The Bell Inn, The Talbot, The Flying Horse Inn, St Peter's Church, St Mary's Church, Cock and Hoop, Old Angel Inn, The Weekday Cross, including many buildings which are often overlooked in our busy lives. I strongly urge anyone to take a moment and just look   up.

Robin Hood

Well, I couldn't really write a book about the history of Nottingham without adding the name Robin Hood, or

Robin of Loxley, but here we are, Robin Hood has long been associated with the town of Nottingham as an outlaw, I don't think I need to explain more about who he was. However, similarities can be found between the efforts of Robin Hood and those of George Smith.

Acknowledgements

Once again, the husband, Phill, who has proved a valuable tool with mapping 1812 Nottingham, thank you for your added support throughout.

Lylah, Rubie and Kal-El Johnson, my three children, without whom I would've completed this work a year ago.

The people of Clifton, you all know who you are, thank you so much for all of your kind words and encouragement, it has been a godsend to have such a wonderful community on my doorstep, a community which never fails, and a community I will always be proud to be a part of.

I will be forever grateful to my neighbours, who have seen me from start to finish throughout the current pandemic, (yes, I mentioned the pandemic in an unrelated book,) you have been our saviours through this.

A special credit to the Nottingham historical societies all references within the book can be found here:

Nottinghamshire History which can be found at
www.nottshistory.org.uk

Nottinghamshire heritage gateway which can be found at
www.nottsheritagegateway.org.uk

St James cemetery which can be found at
www.stjamescemetery.co.uk

The British Newspaper archives.
georgianera.wordpress.com

And of course, www.mumblingnerd.com – Which
contains a very interesting timeline of Nottingham
history.

Nottingham Historical & Archaeological Society

Printed in Great Britain
by Amazon